NASHVILLE - BOOK NINE - YOU, ME
AND A PALM TREE

NASHVILLE - BOOK NINE - YOU, ME AND A PALM TREE

INGLATH COOPER

Contents

Copyright

Books by Inglath Cooper

Swerve
The Heart That Breaks
My Italian Lover
Fences – Book Three – Smith Mountain Lake Series
Dragonfly Summer – Book Two – Smith Mountain Lake Series
Blue Wide Sky – Book One – Smith Mountain Lake Series
That Month in Tuscany
And Then You Loved Me
Down a Country Road
Good Guys Love Dogs
Truths and Roses
Nashville – Part Ten – Not Without You
Nashville – Book Nine – You, Me and a Palm Tree
Nashville – Book Eight – R U Serious
Nashville – Book Seven – Commit
Nashville – Book Six – Sweet Tea and Me
Nashville – Book Five – Amazed
Nashville – Book Four – Pleasure in the Rain
Nashville – Book Three – What We Feel
Nashville – Book Two – Hammer and a Song
Nashville – Book One – Ready to Reach
On Angel's Wings
A Gift of Grace
RITA® Award Winner John Riley's Girl
A Woman With Secrets
Unfinished Business
A Woman Like Annie
The Lost Daughter of Pigeon Hollow
A Year and a Day

Reviews

"If you like your romance in New Adult flavor, with plenty of ups and downs, oh-my, oh-yes, oh-no, love at first sight, trouble, happiness, difficulty, and follow-your-dreams, look no further than extraordinary prolific author Inglath Cooper. Ms. Cooper understands that the romance genre deserves good writing, great characterization, and true-to-life settings and situations, no matter the setting. I recommend you turn off the phone and ignore the doorbell, as you're not going to want to miss a moment of this saga of the girl who headed for Nashville with only a guitar, a hound, and a Dream in her heart." – **Mallory Heart Reviews**

"Truths and Roses . . . so sweet and adorable, I didn't want to stop reading it. I could have put it down and picked it up again in the morning, but I didn't want to." – **Kirkusreviews.com**

On Truths and Roses: "I adored this book…what romance should be, entwined with real feelings, real life and roses blooming. Hats off to the author, best book I have read in a while." – **Rachel Dove, FrustratedYukkyMommyBlog**

"I am a sucker for sweet love stories! This is definitely one of those! It was a very easy, well written, book. It was easy to follow, detailed, and didn't leave me hanging without answers." – **www.layfieldbaby.blogspot.com**

"I don't give it often, but I am giving it here – the sacred 10. Why? Inglath Cooper's A GIFT OF GRACE mesmerized me; I consumed it in one sitting. When I turned the last page, it was three in the morning." – **MaryGrace Meloche, Contemporary Romance Writers**

5 Blue Ribbon Rating! ". . .More a work of art than a story. . .Tragedies affect entire families as well as close loved ones, and this story portrays that beautifully as well as giving the reader hope that somewhere out there is A GIFT OF GRACE for all of us." — **Chrissy Dionne, Romance Junkies 5 Stars**

"A warm contemporary family drama, starring likable people coping with tragedy and triumph." 4 1/2 Stars. — **Harriet Klausner**

"A GIFT OF GRACE is a beautiful, intense, and superbly written novel about grief and letting go, second chances and coming alive again after devastating adversity. Warning!! A GIFT OF GRACE is a three-hanky read...better make that a BIG box of tissues read! Wowsers, I haven't cried so much while reading a book in a long long time...Ms. Cooper's skill makes A GIFT OF GRACE totally believable, totally absorbing...and makes Laney Tucker vibrantly alive. This book will get into your heart and it will NOT let go. A GIFT OF GRACE is simply stunning in every way—brava, Ms. Cooper! Highly, highly recommended!" – **4 1/2 Hearts** — **Romance Readers Connection**

"...A WOMAN WITH SECRETS...a powerful love story laced with treachery, deceit and old wounds that will not heal...enchanting tale...weaved with passion, humor, broken hearts and a commanding love that will have your heart soaring and cheering for a happily-ever-after love. Kate is strong-willed, passionate and suffers a bruised heart. Cole is sexy, stubborn and also suffers a bruised heart...gripping plot. I look forward to reading more of Ms. Cooper's work!" – **www.freshfiction.com**

Reviews

Readers who have enjoyed the emotional stories of authors like Colleen Hoover may enjoy this live-your-dream story where "Inglath Cooper draws you in with her words and her amazing characters. It is a joy to pick up these books. There is just the right amount of love and romance with the perfect dose of reality. The dialogue is relatable and you just fall in love with the story."

♪

"Truths and Roses . . . so sweet and adorable, I didn't want to stop reading it. I could have put it down and picked it up again in the morning, but I didn't want to." – **Kirkusreviews.com**

On Truths and Roses: "I adored this book...what romance should be, entwined with real feelings, real life and roses blooming. Hats off to the author, best book I have read in a while." – **Rachel Dove, FrustratedYukkyMommyBlog**

"I am a sucker for sweet love stories! This is definitely one of those! It was a very easy, well written, book. It was easy to follow, detailed, and didn't leave me hanging without answers." – **www.layfieldbaby.blogspot.com**

"I don't give it often, but I am giving it here – the sacred 10. Why? Inglath Cooper's A GIFT OF GRACE mesmerized me; I consumed it in one sitting. When I turned the last page, it was three in the morning." – **MaryGrace Meloche, Contemporary Romance Writers**

5 Blue Ribbon Rating! ". . .More a work of art than a story. . .Tragedies affect entire families as well as close loved ones, and this story portrays that beautifully as well as giving the reader hope that somewhere out there is A GIFT OF GRACE for all of us." — **Chrissy Dionne, Romance Junkies 5 Stars**

"A warm contemporary family drama, starring likable people coping with tragedy and triumph." 4 1/2 Stars. — **Harriet Klausner**

"A GIFT OF GRACE is a beautiful, intense, and superbly written novel about grief and letting go, second chances and coming alive again after devastating adversity. Warning!! A GIFT OF GRACE is a three-hanky read...better make that a BIG box of tissues read! Wowsers, I haven't cried so much while reading a book in a long long time...Ms. Cooper's skill makes A GIFT OF GRACE totally believable, totally absorbing...and makes Laney Tucker vibrantly alive. This book will get into your heart and it will NOT let go. A GIFT OF GRACE is simply stunning in every way—brava, Ms. Cooper! Highly, highly recommended!" – **4 1/2 Hearts — Romance Readers Connection**

"...A WOMAN WITH SECRETS...a powerful love story laced with treachery, deceit and old wounds that will not heal...enchanting tale...weaved with passion, humor, broken hearts and a commanding love that will have your heart soaring and cheering for a happily-ever-after love. Kate is strong-willed, passionate and suffers a bruised heart. Cole is sexy, stubborn and also suffers a bruised heart...gripping plot. I look forward to reading more of Ms. Cooper's work!" **– www.freshfiction.com**

★

A Contemporary Romance set in the heart of country music. . .Nashville.

"You think you know what matters in life. Chasing after a dream. Catching it. Holding onto it. Fighting for it, if necessary. Until everything comes to a jolting halt, and you get it. Finally, you get it when it becomes crystal clear that everything you thought mattered doesn't matter at all, unless you have the one thing that really does."

For Holden Ashford, this is CeCe, the love of his life. When she's left reeling from an act of violence that abruptly points their lives in another direction, CeCe is no longer sure of the career she's gone after heart and soul. Holden begins to wonder if she is sure of him as well.

Temptation has a way of finding us when we're at our weakest point. And when country superstar Jacob Bartley sets his sights on CeCe, love will be put to its ultimate test.

Holden

YOU THINK YOU know what matters in life. Chasing after a dream. Catching it. Holding onto it. Fighting for it, if necessary.

Until everything comes to a jolting halt, and you get it. Finally, you get it. And it becomes crystal clear that everything you thought mattered, doesn't matter at all, unless you have the one thing that really does.

For me, that's CeCe. My wife. My soul mate. My other half.

I stare at her beautiful face now, reach out and brush the back of my hand across her cheek. Tears well in my eyes, and it feels as if the pain inside me will provide them with permanent fuel, that they will never stop.

The machine monitoring her heart beeps a steady rhythm. Outside the hospital room, I hear the low hum of conversation, punctuated by the occasional staccato of alarm, another person's emergency, another person's pain.

And then I hear CeCe's mom, talking with one of the nurses, repeating questions she's already asked because the answers aren't ones she wants to hear.

"We have no way of knowing how long she will remain unconscious, Mrs. MacKenzie," the nurse responds kindly.

Then Case's voice, asking when they can speak to a doctor.

How did we get here? How did I allow this to happen to CeCe? How did I not realize the danger? Missed the fact that I was putting her at risk. How could I have missed the significance of Charlotte Gearly's actions? How could I have thought there wouldn't be some horrible end to them?

"Baby, I'm so sorry," I say, my voice breaking. "Please wake up. Come back. Please come back. I'm here for you. I'm waiting. I need you so much. Don't leave me. Please don't leave me."

I hear footsteps at the door, raise my head to find Thomas standing there, looking at me with unedited grief on his face. "Hey, man," he says.

"Hey, Thomas," I say, sitting up without bothering to clear the torment from my expression.

He walks over, and I stand up from my chair. He reaches out and clamps me in a hard hug, holding onto me like one brother trying to save another from drowning. I absorb the comfort he's offering because I know that he understands. No one in this world could possibly understand the way he does.

"I'm so sorry, Holden," he says, each word laden with the weight of pure sorrow.

There aren't any other words to cover it. He lets me go after a few moments, pulling back to give me a long look.

"You're going to get through this," he says. "And so will CeCe. You know how strong she is. She's going to be okay."

I want to believe he's right. Dear God, I want to. "What if she's not, Thomas?"

"Don't do that," he says. "She needs your faith. Your strength. You need to give her that."

"How did I let this happen?" I ask, shaking my head.

Misery darkens Thomas's expression, and I suspect he's also blaming himself. "We can't control what another person does, Holden. That girl was sick. Mentally sick. CeCe was a victim of that."

"Our baby was a victim of that," I say, pain rising in me with so much force that my knees buckle, and I sink onto the chair next to the bed, crying under the weight of sorrow. "Maybe that's why she's not waking up. Because she knows our baby is gone."

Thomas puts a hand on my shoulder, gripping hard as if it's the only way he can keep me from slipping into a darker place than the one I'm already in. I don't look up at him, but I can feel the grief shaking through him. It settles in the room around us, a choking blanket of disbelief.

"You're going to get through this, Holden," he says. "Both of you are."

But I don't know if he's right. If CeCe will let herself come back. All I know is that I don't want to be here without her.

I can't be here without her.

♪

THOMAS SITS ON one side of the bed, holding CeCe's hand, and I sit on the other. Neither of us lets go, and we don't talk. I can't find any words that seem capable of expressing what I'm feeling. So I don't try, and neither does he.

At some point, the door to the room opens, and a doctor walks in. The nurses have been in and out constantly, but this is the first time Dr. Walker has been in since early morning. Thomas and I both stand at his entrance but don't let go of CeCe's hands.

Dr. Walker is the most prominent doctor at Vanderbilt for traumatic brain injury. And although he's already assured me CeCe's CT scan looks good, he knows I am beyond terrified by the fact that she hasn't woken up yet.

"She has every reason to come back," Dr. Walker says, looking at me with a sincerity I am grateful for. "Sometimes, a patient needs to resurface at her own speed. Our bodies and brains are far more complex than we can begin to understand. I believe that our brains sometimes protect us from grief and loss in exactly this way. Keep talking to her, telling her things you know she needs to hear. And we will wait."

I nod once, grateful for his assurance, hoping I have the strength to believe it.

♪

TWO DETECTIVES ARRIVE at the hospital late that afternoon. Thomas goes out into the hall to speak with them, coming back in a few moments and saying, "They're insistent on speaking with you now. I'll stay with her, okay?"

I don't want to leave, but I know I'll have to talk with them eventually. I've already put them off several times.

I walk out into the hall where a man and woman dressed in dark clothes are waiting for me. "Mr. Ashford," the woman says, "we'll try not to take too much of your time. We understand what you're going through, but we do need to ask you a few questions. There's a waiting room just down the hall. Maybe we could talk there?"

I nod and follow them to the room that is thankfully empty.

"I'm Detective Aronson," she says, "and this is my partner, Detective Linder. Why don't we sit?"

We take the circle of chairs by the window, and I drop onto the seat, wanting only to get it over with.

"We understand that Charlotte Gearly had been stalking you for some time. Is that correct?"

"That's correct," I say.

"Were you aware that she was in the house?"

The question comes from Detective Linder, and the words contain none of the empathy his partner had just shown.

I lean back a little, trying to assess his angle. "If I had known she was in the house, do you think I would have let her anywhere near my wife?"

"Of course not," Detective Aronson says. "Do you believe she had ever been in the house before?"

"Not to my knowledge, but we know that she stole our dog from our backyard and dropped him a few hours away. I knew she was capable of bad stuff, but I never imagined—"

"We're very sorry, Mr. Ashford," the female detective says softly. "We just need to tie up some loose ends."

I stare at them for a few moments, trying to find words that might in some way be appropriate. But I don't have any. Because the whole thing is just so sad. It's sad that Charlotte Gearly was a sick person who needed help and didn't get it. Sadder still that her actions took from CeCe and me a child we will never have the chance to know.

♪

CeCe

I HEAR HOLDEN calling me.

I want to answer. But something is stopping me. I don't know what it is. It feels as if my brain is being held hostage. Preventing words from surfacing past my lips.

I try to open my eyes. It feels as if they are hinged shut. As if I'm not in control of anything regarding my body.

And there's pain. In my abdomen? Or is it my chest? My heart?

Frustration wells up and settles tight in my throat.

Holden's voice again. I reach for it, struggling to process what I hear in the sound of my name.

He's crying.

What's wrong?

I try to scream the words but they only echo in my head.

He needs me. Holden needs me. I have to get to him. I try to move up, forward. There's a wall in front of me though. I can't push through it.

Why can't I get to him? Panic stabs my chest like a knife. There's an answer. It floats up from somewhere deep inside me. I reach for it, feel it slip through my fingers like water.

I start to sob because I want to know what I'm reaching for. Am I crying out loud? Or is it only in my head?

Why is Holden crying? Why am I crying? What's happened?

And then I remember.

Oh, dear God. I remember.

♪

LIFE GIVES US choices.

Sometimes, they're so small we can't possibly recognize their significance until it's too late. Until the decision is made. And then there is no more choice. Only consequence.

The choice was to think that we could handle the situation with

Charlotte. Assume that she could never really hurt us. And we were wrong.

I don't want to open my eyes. I know Holden is here beside me. I feel him, feel his grief, his love like a cloak waiting to envelop me. If I open my eyes, I will have to let it in. Acknowledge the why of his grief.

Because I know.

Our baby is gone. As soon as full awareness descended over me, I knew.

I'm empty inside. It's the certainty of this emptiness that makes me realize what it meant to have that little life growing within me. The miracle of it. The heartbreaking loss of that life.

I feel Holden take my hand, lace his fingers through mine. Finally, I force myself to open my eyes, and I settle my blurred gaze on his beautiful, grief-stricken face.

He raises his eyes to mine, and I see the fear collapse inside him. He reaches for me, scooping me up and into his arms. I realize there's a cast on my right arm, and it feels like a hard wall between us.

"CeCe. Thank God. Oh, baby. Thank, God."

He begins to cry. And I know I should. The pain inside my chest is like nothing I've ever known. I want the release of tears, but they won't come. I bury my face against his shoulder.

I am numb. Feeling something, anything would be a relief.

But there is nothing. Just blank space where there was once joy, hope, happiness. I can't imagine ever feeling any of those things again.

♪

HOLDEN KEEPS THE police out of the room for nearly twenty-four hours. I hear him arguing with them outside the door a few times. I'm grateful at first, but then reality insists that I can only put it off for so long, and I tell him to let them in. I want to get it over with.

Holden reluctantly agrees, but manages to convince the two detectives waiting to see me that both of them will be too much for me. The woman comes in alone, closing the door behind her, softening her expression as she approaches the bed.

"Hello, Mrs. Ashford. I'm sorry to be meeting you under these circumstances."

"CeCe is fine," I say. "Please, sit down."

"Thank you," she says, pulling a chair to an angle where we are facing each other. "How are you feeling?"

"Better, I guess."

"I wanted to say I'm very sorry about—"

"Thank you," I say, not letting her finish. I don't want to hear token condolences. And then, realizing I'm being unfair to her, add, "How can I help you, detective?"

"We just have a few questions to ask you about Ms. Gearly and the night of the accident."

"It wasn't an accident," I say, hearing the steel in my voice. "Charlotte Gearly came into our home with the intent of harming me so that she could have my husband."

"Incident," she corrects.

"Isn't crime more accurate? She threatened to kill me with a knife and then pushed me down the stairs. She killed our—" I stop there as anger threatens to swallow me whole.

"I'm sorry, Mrs. — CeCe. I don't mean to lessen the significance of what happened. We're just trying to understand the series of events. Can we start at the beginning of the party? I assume you didn't know that Ms. Gearly had gotten a job with the caterer?"

"Of course, I didn't. And I had no idea she was in our home."

"When did you first realize that she was?"

"When she lured me upstairs. She apparently told one of the waitresses to tell me that my mother wanted to see me upstairs."

"What happened when you first walked into the bedroom?"

"She was hiding behind the door. She slammed it shut and waved a knife at me. She threatened to stab me in the stomach with it."

"She knew you were pregnant?"

"I don't know how she knew, but she did. I had only told my husband earlier that night."

The detective writes on her notepad for a minute or more before looking up at me with compassion in her eyes. I can see that she wants to acknowledge the tragedy of what has happened. Her struggle to remain professionally indifferent is obvious. She clears her throat. "We've spoken with her father. The mother hasn't been in her life. Her father had no idea that she was stalking your husband. She lived with him. He's morbidly obese, and she was apparently his caretaker."

The words register. I try to resist their sting, but they settle around me with unwelcome awareness. A picture of Charlotte's life forms in my mind, and I blink hard against it. I don't want to feel sympathy for her. I don't want to imagine the kind of life she must have had.

I will not feel sorry for her.

I won't.

"Detective, I'm really tired. Can we be done here?"

I feel her gaze on me, but refuse to meet her eyes. I don't want her sympathy either. I just want to be left alone.

"I can come back later then," she says, closing her notebook. She stands, hesitates, before adding, "I'm truly sorry for your loss."

As she walks from the room, I realize I should thank her, but I can't force the words past my lips. I turn onto my side and curl into a tight ball. I want to sleep. That is the only time I can escape the pain. That is all I want. Escape.

♪

Holden

CECE IS DIFFERENT.

I see it in her eyes. I feel it in the distance between us.

Dr. Walker releases her three days after she regains consciousness. He's done a long list of tests to make sure they haven't missed anything. He's signing her release forms when he asks to see me in the hall for a moment. I step outside with him, surprised that he had made the request in front of CeCe. But she doesn't seem to notice, her gaze focused on something beyond the room window.

"Her sadness is normal," Dr. Walker says, once we've reached the end of the hall where there's a quiet place to talk. "However, if it goes on beyond what seems expected, I'd like to suggest she see a psychiatrist."

"What do you mean?" I ask, completely caught off guard by the suggestion.

"Holden, your wife has been through a very traumatic experience. Not only did someone try to take her life, but she's also lost a child. It's hard to say what kind of long-term effects this will have on her. It's my hope that she will move through the stages of grief and find peace again somewhere down the road."

"How long can that take?" I ask, hardly knowing where to start.

"Every person is different. I would expect some symptoms of PTSD."

"Post traumatic stress disorder," I say.

"Yes."

"What symptoms?"

"Nightmares. Flashbacks. Negative thinking in someone who used to be a positive person."

"What do I do if—"

Dr. Walker interrupts and puts a hand on my shoulder, his voice assuring when he says, "Let's cross that bridge if we get to it. CeCe seems like a strong young woman. Hopefully, all she will need is time."

I want to believe him. CeCe is strong. I know that. We've both been

9

through hard times, managed to put a shooting behind us. Moved on when moving on seemed impossible.

But we've never lost a child.

♪

CeCe

HOLDEN AND I don't talk throughout the act of leaving the hospital. We get checked out. I wait in a wheelchair with the nurse at the front entrance — all actions that feel way too familiar and make me think about the shooting we had managed to live through.

I blank the memories from my mind, trying to focus on something else. The cast on my arm feels restrictive, and then I'm remembering Charlotte and the stairs and the fall and losing my baby.

This is the thought that feels like a punch in the heart every time I let it surface. Tears well in my eyes, but I blink them back. The nurse notices, pats my arm in sympathy, no words needed. I guess she sees people like me every day.

Holden pulls up in the Range Rover, comes around to help me in and thanks the nurse. I try to smile at her, but it breaks in half, and I look away before the tears follow.

We've just gotten on the highway when Holden reaches across and takes my hand. He locks his fingers with mine, squeezing tight. I stare out the window for a few minutes, and with every mile that leads us closer to home, the air in my chest constricts, tighter and tighter, until I can't breathe.

I press a hand to my chest, feeling as if I'm going to suffocate.

Holden looks at me, alarm in his eyes. "What is it, CeCe? What's wrong?"

"I can't go there."

"Where, hon?"

"Our house. Not yet."

He's silent for a moment, as if he's not sure what to say. "Where do you want to go?" he finally says in a low, caring voice.

I shake my head. "Anywhere. A hotel. It doesn't matter. Just not there."

I sense his confusion and his desire to do what I want. I know I'm scaring him, but I'm just not ready to face our home yet.

"I'll ask Thomas if he and Lila can keep the dogs a couple more days," he says. "We can stay at the Hermitage downtown. That okay?"

"Sure," I say, hearing the neutrality in my voice. I pull my hand from his, locking my palms in my lap and staring straight ahead.

I feel Holden's hurt, and I want to tell him I didn't mean it, but I can't find the strength to push the words past my lips, so we drive in silence.

He calls the hotel, makes a reservation and then calls Thomas to ask about Hank Junior and Patsy staying longer.

I want to see our dogs. Be in the place I've loved and felt safe.

But I don't know if I can ever feel safe there again.

♪

THE HOTEL IS a blanket of luxury, and for twenty-four straight hours, I wrap myself up in it, blanking out the world beyond its walls. I wake up often enough to know that Holden is in the room, not sleeping, watching me. I know he's worried, but I'm not ready to face what I have to face.

Oblivion is the only thing capable of making my thoughts go away. And so every time I start to surface from sleep, I will it back, keeping my eyes closed, not wanting to know what time of day or night it is.

But I hear Holden calling my name at some point. I try to resist answering. Panic begins to edge the plea with which he calls me. I can't ignore it. I have to pull myself up and out.

I turn over and force my eyes open, squinting against the light.

"Babe," he says, sitting down on the edge of the bed and cupping my face with his hand. "You haven't eaten in almost two days. I've ordered some room service. Please. Try to eat something."

I slide up and lean against the bed's headboard, wanting to do as he's suggested. My body feels as if it's been infused with lead, a concrete block on my chest.

"I'm sorry," I say, pushing my hand through my hair and realizing I need a shower.

"You don't need to be sorry," he says. "I'm just really concerned about you."

"I'm okay," I insist.

"You're not," he says, his eyes holding mine and refusing to let me be anything other than honest.

"I will be," I say.

"What can I do, CeCe?" he asks, his voice breaking across my name. "How can I fix this?"

I lean forward and rest my head against his shoulder, drawing in its familiar safety. "No one can fix it, Holden. It's something we have to endure, process, accept. That's the only way to go on, isn't it?"

"We have each other," he says. "We'll get each other through it."

I nod, but my heart isn't convinced. I want it to be, but it isn't.

♪

I FEEL A LITTLE better after a shower, even though it's not easy to manage with a cast on my arm.

I eat the soup Holden has ordered for my lunch. Once I'm done and he has taken the tray away, I have no idea what kind it was. I do not remember the taste of it. He asks me if I liked it and I tell him yes because that's what he needs to hear.

My brain is wide awake now, my thoughts veering from one realization to another. A woman hated me. A woman wanted my husband. A woman caused the death of our baby. That woman is dead. How do we go on?

♪

IF SLEEP CAME willingly before, it will no longer come at all. It's the middle of the night. Holden is asleep beside me, his arm curved around my waist, as if he knows he has to hold onto me even when he's not awake. That to let me go might mean losing me forever.

I stare at the sliver of light stealing through the center of the hotel room curtains. It's the only break in the darkness, and my gaze stays there.

It's dawn when I finally realize that I have to know who Charlotte Gearly was. How she could have done what she did to us.

I wake Holden up and tell him.

♪

Holden

I HAVE TO BELIEVE it isn't a good idea.

I know it isn't.

But it's the first sign CeCe has shown of fighting back against the cloud of anguish she's been submerged beneath since the night Charlotte Gearly upended our lives. If seeing where she lived will somehow help her move forward, I have no choice but to agree.

And so, here we are standing at the door of the apartment where Charlotte lived, according to one of the newspaper articles I read a few days ago. The story had revealed the name of the complex. A scan of the mailboxes on the first floor had shown the name Gearly on apartment 24, the second floor.

I knock at the battered, in-need-of-paint door, insisting that CeCe stand behind me.

A man's voice calls out, "Come in." This seems extremely weird, but I turn the knob and find it unlocked.

"Who is it?" the man asks.

"I'm Holden Ashford," I say. "My wife and I would like to speak to you."

A long silence follows my request. The man finally says, "Come in," the words resigned, as if he has been expecting us and has no choice but to agree.

I take CeCe's hand, and we walk inside the apartment. I close the door behind us. The place smells stale, as if it hasn't been cleaned in a long time. The curtains are drawn, the glare of the TV the only light.

We walk into the living room and see a man sitting in a double-width chair, the television ten feet away. CeCe and I both stare at him. I'm so caught off guard that I can't find anything to say. He is enormous. Rolls of fat form the body that fills the large chair. His head appears small in comparison. He looks beached. Like a whale that has mistakenly ended up on shore with no water to help him back out to the ocean.

"What do you want?" he asks, the question low and weary, almost void of life force but with resentment at its edges.

"We want to ask about your daughter," CeCe says.

"You know she's dead," he says. "What could you possibly want to ask?"

I feel CeCe flinch at the harshness of his words. "Did you know she was stalking us?" I ask, not bothering to soften the question.

He doesn't answer for a bit, and when he does, the resentment seems to be gone from his voice. "Not fully," he says. "I knew she wasn't making wise choices."

This seems the height of irony, coming from him. How could he expect that his daughter would have listened to anything he said regarding choices? "Was she seeing a counselor or a psychiatrist?" I ask.

"I don't know," he says. "But what difference could it possibly make now either way?"

"It makes a difference to us," CeCe says.

He looks directly at her, something in his wide face now revealing his own grief. "I wish I had words to express how sorry I am for what Charlotte did. I can't imagine what she must have been thinking. I'm just sorry for your loss."

Tears well in CeCe's eyes, and she shakes her head a little, as if she has no idea what to say. "I just don't understand why it had to happen," she says. "Why someone didn't realize that Charlotte needed help."

"I guess I should have," he says, not meeting CeCe's tortured gaze. "The truth is Charlotte spent her time taking care of me and not the other way around. Maybe because her life here was so bad, she tried to make up a far better one. Lived in a fantasy world, I mean."

I'm not sure what CeCe hoped to gain in coming here, but I can see that she's torn between anger and pity.

"She could have gone to live with her mother when we divorced," he says. "But she was afraid there wouldn't be anyone to take care of me, so she stayed. That was a mistake. I can see that now. She needed to have a life."

"What are you going to do, Mr. Gearly?" CeCe asks softly.

"What I should have done a long time ago," he says in a self-deprecating voice. "Get back to taking care of myself."

"We should be going, CeCe," I say, reaching for her hand and feeling as if I need to pull her back from the edge of something I can't yet identify.

"Was there a funeral for Charlotte?" she asks.

Mr. Gearly looks down at his hands, shame etching his voice when he says, "No. I couldn't get there, and there really wasn't anyone else to go. Her mother — we haven't heard from her in years."

Shock flashes across CeCe's face, and I know what she's thinking. It's nearly impossible to believe that Charlotte's life could have been that barren of friendship or love. As difficult as it is to let pity in, I feel the sting of it in my heart. And I can see that CeCe does as well.

♪

I HOLD THE DOOR of the Range Rover open, and CeCe slides inside, her face a neutral mask. But as soon as I climb in and start the engine, her control dissolves, and she begins to sob.

I reach for her, wrapping my arms around her as tightly as I dare, wanting to absorb into myself every bit of the anguish she is feeling.

"It's just so horrible," she says, crying against me. "Her life—"

"I know. But you can't let yourself think about it."

"There was no one to go to her funeral. How can that be?"

"I don't know," I say, shaking my head.

"None of this makes sense," she says, trying to stop crying, but the tears only flow faster. "How can I feel sorry for her?"

I pull back and put my hand against her face. "Because that's the kind of heart you have. And that's why I love you so much."

I hold her for a long time, until her sobbing has stopped. She feels weak against me, and I realize that whatever fight had brought her here to see Charlotte's father today is now gone again.

"Where to from here, babe?" I ask. "Can we go home?"

She doesn't answer for a bit, so I wait, letting her make the decision. Finally, she says, "Yes. Please take me home."

♪

CeCe

MAMA GREETS US AT the door when we get to the house. Her face is a flickering mix of worry, sadness and hope. "Come here, sweetheart," she says, pulling me into her arms and hugging me tight.

I hug her back, remembering anew how safe I feel in her arms. How her comfort fills me with the realization that her love is always here. No matter what. Today is no different. Fresh tears well up and spill out. With Mama, I don't have to try to hide my anguish.

She puts one arm around my shoulders, and from the other side, Holden puts his around me too. And they both walk me up the stairs to our bedroom, the stairs I had fallen down and lost our baby.

All the way up, I focus on the fact that I'm safe between these two people I love most in the world. And I'm just grateful for their love. More grateful than I could ever express.

♪

HOLDEN LEAVES US alone in the bedroom, giving me a kiss before saying he'll be back as soon as he picks up Hank Junior and Patsy from Thomas and Lila's house.

Once the door closes behind him, Mama sits down on the bed next to me, taking my hand in hers. "You're going to get through this, honey."

I nod once, wanting to relieve her worry by showing her that I'm strong, but I don't feel strong right now. "We went to see Charlotte's father," I say.

Alarm crosses Mama's face. "Why?" she asks.

"I wanted to know what kind of life she had. What would make her do what she did."

"Did you get answers?" she asks, and I can tell she doesn't think there will be any.

"She lived a pitiful life," I say. "Her father didn't even have a funeral for her."

Mama's gaze reflects surprise. "Why?"

"He said she didn't have friends or family who would have come."

19

"What about him?" Mama asks, angry now.

"He's extremely obese," I say softly. "I don't think he can leave the apartment where he lives. It's just — it's horrible, Mama."

She puts her arms around me and pulls me close. "CeCe, your heart is so big. And I understand why you feel sorry for the girl. No one does what she did unless something in their lives is terribly wrong. But you have to think about you right now. And Holden. You both have your own grief to get through. That's going to take a lot of strength for you both to come out of this still whole."

"But I don't think I am," I say. "It's like a piece of me is gone. The piece that was able to feel joy, look forward to each day."

"And that's to be expected," she says. "You've been through an awful trauma. You and Holden both will have to fight your way back to being happy again."

I rest my head on her shoulder the way I did when I was a little girl. I don't say anything for a long time, and when I do, my voice is nearly a whisper. "What if I don't want to?"

"Then I'm going to be here fighting for you until you do. You're going to be all right again, my sweet girl. It's just going to take some time."

♪

I WAKE UP sometime later to the sound of Hank Junior's barking. It is frantic, and I hear him running through the downstairs of the house, barking this mournful bark that nearly tears my heart out. I start to call him just as Holden opens the bedroom door, and Hank bounds into the room, the frantic look on his face replaced by immediate relief the moment he sees me.

Whining, he leaps onto the bed and starts licking my face. I wrap my arms around him, pulling him to me. "Here I am, Hankie. I'm right here. I'm so glad you're home too."

Holden sits beside us on the bed. "Thomas said he's been a wreck. They didn't want to give us anything else to worry about so they've been doing everything they could think of to help him. The vet finally gave him a sedative, but Thomas said that didn't even help. He needed his girl."

Tears well up and slide down my face. "You're my good boy," I say. "Everything is okay."

Holden reaches out and brushes his hand across my hair. "I know exactly how he feels," he says softly. "We both need our girl."

"I'm sorry," I say, unable to stop my tears.

"What do you have to be sorry for?" he asks softly.

"I've made this all about me. I'm sorry for being so selfish."

"CeCe. Baby. I'm going to be okay when you're okay. You're my world. You know that. Without you, nothing I do or have makes any sense at all. We'll get through this. Together."

I nod, wanting to give him the comfort and strength he's been giving me. But I'm empty. As I have never before been. And I have absolutely nothing to give.

♪

Holden

A WEEK PASSES, each day a new chance for me to see that CeCe is going to be all right. I know she's not sleeping well, and one night I wake up aware that she is awake beside me.

"Can't sleep?" I say, rolling over and pulling her to me, her back to my chest.

She doesn't answer for a moment, and when she does, her voice is decisive, as if she's been awake for a good while, thinking. "I want to help him."

"Who?" I ask.

"Her father."

"Mr. Gearly?"

"Yes."

I don't know exactly what to say. I'm not surprised that she's been thinking about him. I have too, actually. "How would we do that?"

"I don't know," she says quietly. "But don't you think he'll sit there and die if someone doesn't?"

"I don't know, babe."

"I wish I could just feel anger for what she did. But after seeing him, seeing where she lived and what her life must have been like, I feel sorry for her too. I have plenty of anger. But I also know that the only way back to peace is forgiveness. It's the hardest possible thing to do, but maybe it's the only way to be close to whole again."

"He might not want our help."

"Then at least we'll know we tried."

"Okay," I say, and then because I know she needs this step forward, I add, "We'll go see him in the morning?"

"Yes," she says.

And a few minutes later, she is asleep in my arms.

♪

CeCe

WE GET TO Mr. Gearly's apartment at just after ten. Mama had offered to come with us, but I think this is something Holden and I need to do alone. He holds my hand going up the stairs. My heart is pounding by the time we reach the door and knock.

The voice that calls out, "Come in," is a much weaker voice than the one we heard a week ago.

Holden opens the door, and we go inside. The apartment smells even worse than before, and I'm overcome with the desire to open windows, let in fresh air.

Mr. Gearly is sitting in the same chair. The TV isn't on this time though. One glance at him makes it clear he is in bad shape. His lips look parched, and his large face is deathly pale.

I drop onto my knees beside his chair. "Mr. Gearly, are you sick?"

"You shouldn't be here," he says, shaking his head and refusing to open his eyes.

"We're here to help you," I say softly, putting my hand over his enormous one.

"You can't help me," he says. "No one can."

"We can if you let us, sir," Holden says, standing behind me with his hand on my shoulder.

"I just want to die," he says, the words low and insistent. "Please, go. Just let me die here. That's the best thing that can happen."

"Mr. Gearly," I say, my throat tight, "I know it must feel that way right now. But that's not what your daughter would have wanted."

He's quiet for a few moments, and, with his eyes still closed, finally says, "If I had just died a long time ago, maybe she wouldn't have done the awful things she did."

"We have no way of knowing that," I say. "But I believe that we have to try to go on in the best way that we can. Find a way to put some good back into the world."

He does open his eyes then, looking at me with the saddest

expression I have ever seen. "I don't know if that's possible when you've lived a life of mistakes."

"With the next moment, we have another chance to do differently."

"You really believe that?"

"I do."

"You're an amazing young woman, you know that?"

"No," I say, shaking my head. "Just trying to find my way like everyone else."

"When was the last time you had food or water, Mr. Gearly?" Holden asks.

"I don't know," he says, and I wonder if he's had anything since the last time we were here. "We're going to get you to the hospital, and we'll start from there, okay, Mr. Gearly?"

He closes his eyes again, and tears slide between his lids and over his full cheeks. He nods then, once, out of defeat or out of gratitude, I don't know.

♪

Holden

A TEAM OF paramedics arrive within ten minutes of our call. I had stepped outside the apartment to dial 911, not wanting Mr. Gearly to hear the conversation because I wanted to prepare them for the fact that it was going to be difficult getting him out of the apartment and down the stairs.

But even I had underestimated the difficulty of it.

The first paramedic through the door recognizes CeCe and me immediately, judging from the look on his face. But he quickly wipes the surprise from his face, replacing it with committed professionalism.

"How can we help you folks today?" he asks, his glance sweeping the room and landing on Mr. Gearly.

"I think our friend, Mr. Gearly, needs to be admitted to the hospital," CeCe says then. "We don't know how long he's been without food or water."

The paramedic nods once and walks over to Mr. Gearly's chair, squatting down beside him and putting a hand on his arm. "Mr. Gearly? We're going to help you, sir. Can you tell me if you're in any kind of pain?"

He shakes his head and says, "No."

"Okay, that's good. We're going to go ahead and start an IV, get some fluids in you and see if we can get you to feeling a little better. We'll get you over to Vanderbilt then and let those good folks help you."

Mr. Gearly nods once, then looks at CeCe and me and says, "Thank you. Thank you."

♪

CeCe

IT IS ALL I can do to stand quietly at the bottom of the stairs while five paramedics and Holden carry Mr. Gearly down the stairs on a wide stretcher. I can see the strain of the effort on their faces, and I can only hope that none of them will be hurt or that they will drop him.

I all but hold my breath until they reach the last step and walk the stretcher the dozen or so feet to the ambulance, which has been backed up as close as possible to the apartment building, its red lights flashing.

Once they have him inside, Holden and I get into the Ranger Rover and follow the vehicle onto the street. He reaches across and takes my hand. It feels as if we're both breathing a sigh of relief.

"Do you think he'll be okay?" I ask.

"I hope so," he says. "I don't know though. He seems to be in bad shape."

"I wish we'd come sooner."

"We didn't know, babe."

I nod, but it's hard to think of him sitting there all those days, trying to die. "It's just so sad," I say.

"It is," he agrees.

"How do these things happen to people, Holden?"

He doesn't answer for a few moments, and then he says, "A combination of circumstances and choices? Some people definitely have harder things happen to them, things that don't seem fair. But maybe it's about how we choose to respond to those things. To keep fighting. Or not."

I look at his handsome face, and for the first time since that awful night, feeling flutters in my heart. "Have I told you lately that I love you?"

He locks his fingers with mine, squeezes tight. "You have no idea how much I needed to hear that."

"I do love you, Holden."

"I know. And I love you."

♪

WE'VE BEEN AT the hospital for almost two hours when a doctor finally comes out to talk to us. His expression is stern and no-nonsense, as if he really doesn't have time to come out to the waiting room but is obligated to do so.

Holden and I both stand and shake his hand.

"Dr. Adams," he says.

"I'm CeCe. This is my husband, Holden."

"I know who you are," he says, and it's clearly not a point in our favor.

"How is he?" I ask, ignoring his curtness.

"He's given me permission to speak with you since I understand you're not family."

"No," Holden says, and I hear the bristle in his voice. "We're just hoping to help him out."

"He's in bad shape, as I'm sure you could tell," Dr. Adams says, modulating his tone.

"Will he be all right?"

"Hard to say at this point. His heart has endured extraordinary stress from the weight alone. We'll give him all the support we can. I'm afraid it's a wait-and-see thing. I would suggest you come back tomorrow. Let's see how he does overnight."

I want to argue, insist that we stay, but it's not really our place. "Okay," I say. "Thank you."

He turns and leaves the room then without another word.

"Was it my cologne?" Holden asks once he's gone.

I shake my head. "Maybe he hates country music."

"His loss," Holden says.

"We'll come back in the morning," I say. "Do you think he has the will to fight?"

"I don't know," he says honestly. "That's the part no one else can do for him."

♪

Holden

WE'RE WALKING OUT the main entrance of the hospital when I spot the reporters. Three of them with camera guys and microphones.

"Holden! CeCe!" one of the female reporters calls out, running toward us in high heels. "May we have a quick word?"

I reach for CeCe's hand and get between her and the reporters. "We really have to get home," I say, giving the woman a cool smile.

"Just a couple of questions," she says.

CeCe pulls me to a stop and says, "About what?"

"When can we expect to see you on tour again?" she asks, smiling a wide white smile.

"We're working out the details of that," I answer. "No definite date yet."

"Any new songs coming out soon?"

"Yeah," I say. "New stuff being released next month."

"I know your fans will be thrilled to hear that," she says, and then the smile disappears. "We understand you were here today with the father of your stalker, Charlotte Gearly. You must admit that seems a little curious, given the circumstances."

Clearly the tour and music questions had been a lead-up to this. "We have to go, ma'am," I say, taking CeCe's hand and walking away.

"He's apparently obese," she calls out after us. "And we understand the daughter had been taking care of him. Why would you be here with him after what she did to you?"

CeCe stops and turns around, staring at the woman long and hard before saying, "Do you believe that people sometimes do something just because it's the right thing?"

The reporter smiles her bleached smile and says, "Not very often."

"He needs help," CeCe says. "We're helping him. End of story."

And we walk away.

♪

IT MUST BE A slow news day because the story is on the six o'clock

31

news that evening. CeCe and I are in the kitchen with her mom, who is putting together dinner for us. She likes to watch the news on the kitchen TV while she's cooking.

I instantly recognize the reporter's voice and look up to see our faces on the screen. They edit our answers to her questions so that it ends up sounding like we have something to hide.

"We shouldn't have talked to her," CeCe says, putting down the knife she'd been using to dice an onion.

"Don't pay any attention to her, honey," Mrs. MacKenzie says. "Honestly, they can be such leeches."

I walk over and slip my arms around CeCe's waist, kiss her on the neck. "Your mom's right, you know."

"Can people actually try to do something good without being suspected of having some evil ulterior motive?" she asks, and I hear the frustration in her voice.

"They ought to be able to," I say. "But she's got sensationalism to sell. Don't let it get to you, babe."

"I know. That just makes her effective."

My cell rings. I pull it from my back pocket to see Thomas's grinning face on the screen. I take the call, saying, "Hey. What's up?"

"We just saw the news. What's going on?"

I open the door to the backyard and walk outside. Hank Junior and Patsy scoot out behind me, trotting across the stone terrace to the grass.

"CeCe and I went to see Charlotte's dad after CeCe got out of the hospital. It was really awful, man. I guess she must have taken care of him. He's so overweight he can't take care of himself. I guess CeCe has been thinking about him. She wanted to go back and try to get him some help. When we got there, he was in bad shape. I don't know how long he'd been without food or water. Apparently, he had canceled the nurse's aide who had been coming in after Charlotte died."

"That's some unreal stuff," Thomas says, his tone disbelieving. "You could almost feel sorry for her if she hadn't caused so much pain."

"I know. The whole thing seems tragic on so many levels."

"How is CeCe?"

"She's doing okay. We haven't talked much about the miscarriage. I want to but I don't think she's ready."

"Give her time. She has a lot of healing to do. You both do. You know if there's anything we can do, all you have to do is ask. We're here for you in whatever way we can be."

"Thanks, Thomas. That means a lot."

"Maybe y'all ought to get away for a little while. Get some distance from everything that's happened."

"It's probably not a bad idea. CeCe didn't want to come home at first. She didn't think she could be here again."

"That sucks. Your home ought to be the one place you feel safe. Hey, Holden?"

"Yeah?"

"You two need to take care of each other."

"We will," I say.

"When you're ready to work on some new music, let me know. That's always been a good place for you to go."

"Thanks, Thomas. Give Lila and Lexie a kiss for me."

"Will do."

I stand there in the grass for a while after we hang up, thinking about what Thomas had said. For the first time, I let myself wonder if our baby was a boy or a girl. Would he or she have looked like me or CeCe? Both of us? Would he or she have loved music?

Grief crashes against my heart in a fresh wave.

♪

CeCe

MAMA'S ON THE phone with Case when I look out the kitchen window for Holden. He's standing with his back to the house, but I can see his shoulders shaking, and I know he's crying.

This picture of him opens a crack in my heart. My hand goes to my belly, and grief for the child that is no longer there floods through me.

I want to go to him, pull him into my arms, offer comfort, be comforted. But somehow, I can't make myself open the door and walk across the grass to him. I feel empty, as if I have no reservoir of sympathy to share with him. I feel selfish. This isn't my loss only. It's our loss. And I know it's one we should share together.

I feel the chasm between us, a crack in our foundation that has never been there before. It scares me. I want to deny its existence, step over it into familiar territory. But it is as if my arms and legs have been infused with lead. I can't make myself open the door and go to him. I can only turn away and close my eyes against the image of his sorrow.

♪

THE NEXT MORNING, I'm awake with the sun. I get up and make coffee, let Hank Junior and Patsy outside, where they sniff all the new sniffing spots that popped into existence overnight.

I sit on the terrace and watch them trot from one location to the next, tails wagging all the while. I think how simple and complete their happiness is, living in the moment, nothing from the past or the future to weigh them down.

I can't help but wish we humans had the ability to live like that. But we bring our past into the present, and that inevitably shapes our future.

I take a sip of the hot coffee, noticing the taste doesn't appeal to me as it usually does. Food in general hasn't tasted the same since I left the hospital, my appetite more of a forced effort than any real desire to eat.

I think of Mr. Gearly and wonder how he is this morning. I can't imagine what it would be like to have absolutely no one in the world to care what happened to me. To give me the will to go on even when I didn't want to.

I call Hank Junior and Patsy to come inside and then go upstairs to get dressed. I'm quiet, and Holden doesn't wake up. I write a note for him and Mama, put it on the kitchen counter and leave the house.

♪

THE DOOR TO his room is closed. I knock once, and when there's no answer, stick my head inside. "Mr. Gearly?"

The light in the room is low, but I can see that his eyes are open, fixed on the wall in front of him.

"You should have let me die in that chair," he says in a voice so soft I can barely hear him. "I don't have anything left to offer this world."

"I don't believe that," I say, walking over to sit on the chair next to the bed.

"It's the truth."

"The truth can change. I believe we make our truth."

He finally lets his gaze meet mine, his eyes filled with a torment that must be impossible to bear.

"Would you believe it if I told you I never in my wildest dreams imagined my life would end up like this?"

"Yes, I would."

"I actually used to play football in college."

"What position?"

"Linebacker. Hurt my knee junior year and lost my scholarship. I didn't come from much, and finding the money to pay for tuition seemed like something that just wouldn't happen."

"What did you do then?"

"I started driving a truck. It was something that didn't put stress on my knee, and I could handle the long distances. But I was used to eating a lot, playing football, and I guess when I quit all that exercise, everything changed. After I got married, I had an even harder time controlling the weight gain. My wife was a good cook. When I was home, I took advantage of it."

"You're not the only person in the world this has happened to, Mr. Gearly."

"Maybe not. But I let it break up my marriage. And ruin my daughter's life."

"Don't say that," I say. "She needed help. And you didn't know."

"I should have. I was too absorbed with my own misery though."

"Maybe it's time to make up for that."

He looks over at me then, his eyes imploring. "What do you mean?"

"By getting better, the fact that she took care of you won't be a waste."

"I'm not trying to be rude by asking this question, but why would you care? After what she did to you and your husband?"

I consider my answer for a few moments before saying, "Because I believe that a wrong will never fix a wrong. Only a right can do that."

♪

A NURSE COMES in and asks me if I can leave the room while they administer some medicine. She smiles at me, says she's a big fan and looks sorry for asking me to leave. I tell Mr. Gearly I'll check on him later. He thanks me, and I can tell he won't be surprised if I never come back.

Outside in the hallway, I see the doctor Holden and I had spoken with yesterday. I walk up to him and ask him for an update.

Dr. Adams looks up from the chart he's scribbling notes on and gives me an assessing look before saying, "Surprisingly better than I would have expected."

"That's wonderful."

"May I ask you a question, Ms. Ashford?"

"Sure," I say.

"Is this like some pet project you're going to lose interest in before long? Because if it is, I think you're doing Mr. Gearly a disservice by making him think you're going to be around when he's trying to figure out where to go from here."

I feel the sting of the words like a slap across the face. I force myself to count to five before I answer. "Do you have any idea how quickly your indifference can crush a person's will to fight?"

"I'm not indifferent, Ms. Ashford. But this man has a real fight ahead of him. And as far as I can tell, it's one he'll be waging without family. It seems unfair to me that you would get his hopes up."

"I am not trying to get his hopes up," I say, reaching the end of my patience. "I'm trying to help him. Since when did that become a crime?"

"It's not a crime, Ms. Ashford. Just highly unusual for someone in your position."

"And what position is that, Dr. Adams?"

"A position of affluence."

"So because I've achieved some level of success, I'm incapable of an act of kindness?" I'm angry now, and I feel the heat of it in my face.

"I would say this goes a little beyond a simple act of kindness."

"You know, Dr. Adams, I genuinely feel sorry for you. I don't know what you've seen in this world to make you so jaded or so suspicious of another person's motives. Whatever it is, I hope you figure it out and let it go, or for the rest of your career, your patients are going to pay the price for it."

My voice has risen, and people have stopped in the hall to turn and look. I walk away from Dr. Adams and hope they heard every word.

♪

CeCe

I RECEIVE A text from Mama right after I get in the car.

Case asked me to come over today. If you're okay, I'll be there for a bit.

I text her back.

I'm fine. You two have a good time. I love you.

I love you, honey.

I lean my head against the seat and close my eyes. I try to figure out what I'm feeling, but the only word I can find for it is numb. It feels as if my life has been rolling along on a track I was completely happy to follow. And now it has come to an abrupt halt.

I have no desire to move forward. Go left or right.

For as long as I can remember, I've known what I wanted in life. Music. And once I met Holden, love. The music is something we've shared, made our bond that much deeper.

But now, it's as if a switch has been turned off inside me, and the music has gone silent. I can't hear it anymore. There's no song inside me.

I think of the counselor I had seen for a while after the shooting. I don't want to go and see her. But I know enough to realize that I should.

I pick up my phone again, scroll through the contacts until I find her name and tap call.

♪

Holden

THE ROOM IS dark when I wake up. I squint at the clock next to the bed, amazed that's it's after ten. I realize the blackout curtains are drawn, and that must be why I've slept so long. CeCe and I use them sometimes when we've been on tour and need some extra sleep.

I get up, take a fast shower and head downstairs. Hank Junior and Patsy are the only ones in the kitchen. I give them each a rub on the head and call out for CeCe. "Babe, are you here?"

When there's no answer, I spot the note on the counter. I pick it up and read her neat handwriting. *Back later. Love you. CeCe*

I pick up my phone, tap her name on the call screen, but voice mail picks up immediately. I glance outside and see that her car and her mom's car are both gone.

I send CeCe a text, asking her to call me, and when there's no response after a minute or so, I call Thomas.

"Hey," he says on the first ring.

"Hey. CeCe over there?"

"No. Why?"

"I slept late, and she's out. Just thought she might have come over to visit with Lila."

"Everything all right?"

"Yeah. She's just struggling with this whole thing."

"Are you worried about her?"

"I don't think so. I don't know. Maybe."

"Come over. I'll make you some coffee."

"Okay. Be there in a few."

Ten minutes later, I let the dogs out of the Rover's back seat, and we meet Thomas at his front door. Brownie is next to him, wagging his tail so hard at the sight of Hank Junior and Patsy that it's basically a blur.

"Come on in," Thomas says. "Lila took Lexie for a haircut. It's just me and Brownie. We'll let the buddies play out back."

Once the dogs are outside, trotting around one after another,

Thomas puts a coffee mug on the counter and pours me a cup from the pot he's already made. "Thanks," I say. "Smells good."

Thomas pulls out a couple of stools at the counter, and we sit down.

"How are you?" he asks.

"Okay, I guess. It just feels like life's been turned upside down. The way it did after the shooting."

"I remember the feeling, man. There's just so much to process. The worst part for me was the realization that another human being wanted to actually hurt me. Kill me. You remember that feeling?"

I nod. Because I do. It's horrible.

"I suspect that's what CeCe's going to have to deal with. This is the second time it's happened to her, and it wasn't only her, but also the child you two made together."

"I know." We're both quiet for a few moments, and then, I say, "She seems all right, Thomas. But maybe she's just trying to be strong for me."

"If that's the case, it won't work. Grief is something we have to swim through to get to the other side."

I take a sip of the coffee, thinking about that. "I still can't believe it happened. It's just so messed up. I'm so angry at Charlotte, but at the same time, I feel beyond sorry for her. How do you sync those two things?"

"I'm not sure you do. Maybe you have to come to terms with them individually."

"Is that even possible?"

"That I don't know, friend."

♪

CeCe

HAZEL McCORMACK LOOKS exactly like my fourth-grade math teacher, Mrs. Arlington. She has short red hair, cut in a pixie style. Her eyes are Irish green with flecks of gold in them. She's also as no-nonsense as Mrs. Arlington, a get-to-the-point kind of person whose sole aim is to get the problem solved. I'm her current problem.

It's eleven o'clock when she leads me into her office and shuts the door behind us. "Thank you so much for working me in, Dr. McCormack. I hope it wasn't an imposition."

"Not at all, dear. It just so happened I had a cancellation, and you know I'm always glad to see you. Please sit down."

I take a seat on her extremely deep sofa, my feet just barely touching the floor.

"I read about the tragedy at your home. First, I'm so sorry that happened to you and your husband."

I nod, looking down at my hands. "Thank you. It's been pretty awful."

"Was it true about the miscarriage?"

I nod again, this time silent.

"I'm so very sorry."

"Thank you."

"Is that why you're here today?"

"I don't know. I guess so."

"Tell me how you're feeling, CeCe."

"Empty."

"Can you tell me about that?"

I shrug, looking out her paned window at a stretch of green grass. The park-like area contains benches where two young women are sitting and chatting while their toddlers play together. "Sort of like I'm not sure what the point is anymore."

"To life? Your work? Your marriage?"

"I love my husband. He's lost as much here as I have. I just wake up in the morning and wonder where I ever found the motivation to go

43

after a career in music. I even wonder why I thought that would make me happy."

"From the things you've told me," she says, "I think music did make you happy. From the time you were a little girl."

"I know that's true, but it's like I've lost the connection between then and where I am now. I have absolutely no desire to sing. That's never happened to me. Singing for me has always been about joy. To be honest with you, I can't imagine ever feeling joyful again."

"CeCe, your feelings are not uncommon, given what you've been through. Give yourself the right to take some time to heal. Your wounds are so fresh you've barely had time to identify them. Have you talked with Holden about this?"

I shake my head. "I feel like I would be letting him and Thomas down if I said I didn't want to sing anymore."

"Wouldn't they both understand that you're going to need some time to get through this?"

"They would. But I know that music is how they both get through hard times."

"We all have our own ways. If they love you, which I can tell they do, they will give you the time you need."

"What if the joy never comes back?" I ask, looking at her now with tears in my eyes.

"As we've discussed before, part of getting well again is believing that it will happen."

"I want to. But it feels as if I have a concrete block on my chest. It's so heavy that the thought of trying to get out from beneath it seems impossible."

"I understand. That's why we'll work to move it a pound at a time. I think it might be a good idea for you to try an antidepressant for a few months. I know you don't like to take medications, but this might be a time when you could really use the help."

"Can I think about that?" I ask.

"Of course. Do you want to come back tomorrow? I have an opening in the afternoon."

"Yes," I say. "Thank you, Dr. McCormack."

"I'm glad you called, CeCe. Sometimes, it's easier not to reach out when we're hurting. The fact that you did tells me how much you want to feel better."

"I do," I say. Even though from here, I have no idea how I will get there.

♪

Holden

I'M GETTING READY to head home when Thomas's cell phone rings. He answers, signaling for me to wait until he's done before I leave. He listens for a moment, and says, "Hey, Jacob. What's up, man?"

I'm wondering Jacob "Who" when Thomas lip mouths, "Bartley."

Jacob Bartley. I raise my eyebrows. He made it big a few years after Case and is known for having a knack for reinventing his sound often enough to keep it interesting. Wonder why he's calling Thomas.

When it looks as if the conversation is going to go on for a bit, I write a note for Thomas and tell him I'm going home to see if CeCe is back. He nods, and I wave Hank Junior and Patsy to the front door, giving Brownie a rub before leaving him inside.

I'm relieved to see that CeCe's car is in the driveway when I pull in. The dogs beat me to the front door, and I call out for her as we step inside.

"Up here," she calls back from our bedroom.

I take the stairs two at a time. She's in bed, raising up on one elbow to squint at me. "Hey."

"Hey," I say softly, sitting down beside her and running a hand across her hair. "I was getting a little worried."

"I went to the hospital to see Mr. Gearly."

"How is he?" I ask.

"A little improved this morning. We talked a bit. That Dr. Adams is determined to run me off though."

"Do I need to talk to him?" I ask, remembering how unpleasant he'd been yesterday.

"I think he got the message from me," she says.

"Good girl."

This brings a hint of a smile to her mouth, but only a hint.

"I also went to see Dr. McCormack."

This surprises me, and I don't do a very good job of hiding it. "You did?"

"Yeah."

"Why?"

"I'm just feeling a little sad."

"I'm sorry, honey," I say, sliding onto the bed beside her and pulling her into my arms. "What can I do?"

"Hold me."

"All day long. All night long."

She presses a kiss to my chest. "She thought I should consider an antidepressant for a few months."

I pull back and look down at her, surprised. "She did?"

"Yeah."

"What do you think?"

"I told her I'd like to think about it."

"What can I do, babe?"

"Just keep loving me."

"That's easy. I want to take away your pain though."

She slides her arms around my neck and kisses me. I feel her need to blank out everything that has happened. More than anything, I want to do that for her.

She starts to unbutton my shirt, slipping her hand inside. I lift her onto my lap, running my hands up the back of her blouse. She makes a soft sound of wanting and deepens the kiss. I tangle my hands in her long hair, and time seems to go still as we kiss and hold onto each other in the quiet of our bedroom.

The instant I feel her tears, it's as if a knife has been driven through the center of my heart. The pain is so intense I can barely breathe. "CeCe," I say, broken.

"Don't stop," she says softly. "Please, Holden. Don't stop. I need you so much."

And now tears are falling down my own face. They melt into hers. She pushes my shirt from my shoulders, and I pull her blouse over her head, tossing it onto the floor. She unhooks her bra, and drops it too. With familiar movements, we lose the rest of our clothes, until we are skin to skin beneath the silk sheets of our bed, soul to soul in acknowledged pain.

She pulls me to her, and then I remember. "CeCe, I don't want to hurt you."

"It's okay. The doctor said two weeks."

"Are you sure?"

She nods, and we blank out everything else except our love for each other, and the rightness of the way our bodies fit together. I want her more than I have ever wanted her. We make love to each other. And it is exactly that. Both of us, hearts broken, wanting to make the other whole again.

♪

CeCe

I'M STILL LYING in bed, warm from Holden's touch, when his phone rings. He's in the shower, so I glance at the screen and see that it's Thomas. I answer with, "Hey, stranger."

"Hey, honey. How are you?"

I hear the very real concern in his voice and wonder what Holden has told him. I brighten my answer because there's no need for him to be worrying about me. "Getting better," I say.

"We miss you. Lila wants to fix dinner for you as soon as you feel like coming over."

"I'd like that. Everybody good there?"

"Yeah," he says, gratitude in his voice. "Really good. Holden told me what you're doing for Charlotte's father."

"You think I'm crazy?"

"No."

"I just needed to change the focus somehow."

"You're amazing."

"Enough about me. What's up?"

"Well, right before Holden left this morning, I got a call from Jacob Bartley."

Holden walks into the room just then, a towel around his waist, his hair wet. "It's Thomas," I say, putting him on the speakerphone.

"Hey," Holden says. "You missing me already?"

Thomas snorts a laugh. "I was missing CeCe."

"So what did Jacob Bartley want?" I ask.

"He'd like to meet with us tomorrow at his studio."

"Why?" Holden asks, sitting down beside me on the bed and taking my hand.

"He didn't want to say over the phone. Said he'd like to have the chance to present it to us in person."

"Interesting," Holden says.

"I know the timing's not great," Thomas says. "If you want, I can ask him if we can meet down the road."

Holden looks at me, and I know I'm the one to make the decision. I don't want to disappoint either one of them or keep them from a good opportunity, so I say, "Tomorrow is fine. What time?"

♪

Holden

WE'RE ON THE way to Bartley's studio the next morning, when I finally ask CeCe what I've been wanting to ask her. "You're doing this for Thomas and me, aren't you?"

She glances out the window, her voice neutral when she says, "I want to be honest with you about how I'm feeling. The only way I can explain it is numb. It seems like the best thing to do is go ahead with life the way we normally live it. And maybe at some point, it will start to feel right again."

I reach across and take her hand, linking my fingers with hers. "Just keep telling me how you're feeling. Don't shut me out. Promise me you won't?"

"I won't," she says, meeting my gaze with a half-smile.

She turns the radio on. The Highway on XM is playing "Amazed," CeCe's voice suddenly filling the car, pure and beautiful. Without hesitating, she changes the station.

♪

BARTLEY'S STUDIO IS in the heart of Music Row. It's one of the largest and most visible. The building, one story and square, is painted a bright red. The shutters are yellow, and an enormous sculpture of a cowboy hat sits prominently in the front yard.

It seems a bit showy to me, but I suppose if you've reached his level of success in Nashville, you can do what you want with your studio.

We park in the side lot. Thomas pulls in behind us in a new black Ford truck. He gets out first, opening CeCe's door for her.

"Come here, beautiful," he says, lifting her up so that her feet aren't touching the pavement.

He holds her like that for several long moments. If anyone understands the bond between them, it's me. I'm grateful for how much he cares.

When he finally lowers her to the ground, his eyes are moist, and he wipes the back of his hand across them. "I can't stand what's happened to you two."

"I know," CeCe says, putting a hand on his arm. "We're getting there."

"If you don't want to be here today, CeCe," he says, "we can cancel this."

"I want to be. I need the distraction."

"You sure?"

"I'm sure."

The main door to the studio opens then, and Jacob Bartley appears in the doorway. He's under six feet, but buff as all get-out, and has the kind of commanding presence that tells people he's somebody, whether they already know it or not. He's wearing his signature cowboy hat and boots. I notice that his gaze settles first on CeCe, lingers a bit longer than seems proprietary before his face splits in a smile, and he strides toward us.

"Glad y'all could make it," he throws out in a deep country voice. He shakes my hand first, dead-on eye contact, killer grip, as if he knows I caught him staring at CeCe and he wants to assure me he's not after my girl. I'm not sure I'm convinced though.

Thomas shakes his hand. "Thanks for the invite, man."

"Absolutely," Jacob says, turning his gaze to CeCe then. He offers his hand, and she shakes it. I'm watching, and I swear, he's got a major crush on my wife.

"Y'all come in," Jacob says, waving us toward the door. We follow him inside. A pretty young receptionist in a short skirt and boots greets us at the front desk. Jacob tells her not to send him any calls until he gets back with her. She says of course and smiles a perfect white smile.

At the end of a long hallway, Bartley takes a right into a giant office with a big walnut desk and eight or ten Restoration Hardware-type leather chairs. The walls are lined with accolades for his music, and I have to admit the guy has earned his fame in Nashville.

"Y'all have a seat," he says. "Can I get you something to drink?"

"I'm good," Thomas and I say at the same time.

"Bottle of water?" CeCe asks.

"Sure thing," he says, walking over to a stainless refrigerator with a glass door through which small bottles of Pellegrino are visible. He pulls one out and hands it to her with a napkin.

"Thank you," she says.

"You're welcome," he answers without directly meeting her gaze.

He takes a leather chair across from us, sitting forward with his elbows on his knees.

"What can we do for you, Jacob?" I ask then, not so sure about our decision to come here today.

"Well, I won't hold you up any longer than necessary, so I'll just get to the point. I work with an organization that supports an orphanage in Belize down in Central America. They do really great stuff there. I've been twice and spent time with the kids, watched with my own eyes what is done for them with the funding and gifts they receive. I'm getting ready to do a pretty big fundraiser here in town. Reba was headlining it with me, but something major came up and she can't. I was hoping y'all would be interested in taking her place."

"Whoa," Thomas says, sitting back in his chair. "That's quite an honor."

"Yes," CeCe agrees. "Thank you for asking us, Jacob."

"You'd be a real asset to the show," he says. "I know you'd bring in your share of the crowd."

"What's the date?" I ask.

"It's two weeks from tomorrow. That's the catch. It's awfully last minute."

"Can you tell us a little more about the orphanage?" CeCe asks.

"Sure," he says, his voice warming to the question. "It provides care and rehab for abused children. Physical and sexual abuse. Most of them have been abandoned. They usually have about thirty children at a time, anywhere from infants to teens."

"How did you become involved?" I ask.

"I was looking around for something I could get involved in. I was adopted, and I guess it's something I have a passion for. This particular organization does amazing work, and I wanted to help bring attention to it."

"Wow," CeCe says. "That's wonderful. I would love to help."

She looks at me, and I don't manage to hide my surprise. I didn't expect her to want to perform any time soon.

"Holden? Thomas? What do you think?" she asks.

"I'm in," Thomas says.

"Yeah. Sounds awesome," I say.

"Fantastic," Jacob says. "If you have time, I'd love to show you a video of the orphanage I took the last time I was there."

"We would love to see it," CeCe says.

Jacob does a really bad job of hiding how thrilled he is by her response. I feel like I'm watching the beginning of something I need to jump out in front of, stop before it has a chance to get started. But that's crazy. I know CeCe better than anyone in the world. The one thing I know I don't have to question is her commitment to me. I have no idea how I ever got lucky enough to have it, but it's real.

I reach across the space between us and take her hand in mine. "We would love to be a part of it, Jacob."

♪

CeCe

"YOU DON'T LIKE him, do you?"

We're driving home a little while later when I ask Holden the question.

He glances at me, his expression neutral. "I don't really know him."

"No, but he seems like a guy with good intentions."

"Does he?"

I hear the doubt in his voice and wonder where it's coming from. "Do you know something about him that I don't?"

"Just a vibe I got."

"What kind of vibe?"

"That he was into you."

"Holden," I say. "Do you really think it would matter even if he was?"

"No," he says, his tone honest.

"Then why would you let it bother you?"

"Maybe I'm not as confident as I come across."

"You should be, where I'm concerned."

He looks at me then, apology in his eyes. "I know. I'm just being a jerk."

"At least you admit it."

"I get brownie points for that?"

"Depends on what's involved with the brownie points."

"I'm a simple guy," he says, giving me the small grin that always makes my heartbeat pick up.

"I'll keep that in mind," I say.

"Hey," he says, putting his hand on my leg. "I'm sorry. I really was being a jerk."

"You don't need to doubt me, you know."

"I know."

"All right then."

"All right then."

♪

WE GO BY the hospital to see Mr. Gearly.

He looks surprised when we walk into the room, as if each time we leave, he doesn't expect us to come back.

"How are you doing?" I ask, standing at the edge of the bed, Holden just behind me.

"They tell me I'm doing better," he says. "I think I actually believe them."

I'm surprised to hear this, but I see something in his eyes I haven't seen before now. Hope.

"That's wonderful, Mr. Gearly," I say, feeling a gratitude I did not expect to feel.

He's silent, but there's struggle in his expression, and he finally says, "I've thought a lot about what you said. That wrong can't be overcome with more wrong. I don't know why you two felt the need to help me, but I want to thank you for doing so. I don't deserve it. I've made so many mistakes with my life, but I've got another chance now. I don't want to squander that. I'd like to lose the weight I need to lose to get out of this bed and justify what you've done for me."

It's only when he's done that I realize tears are running down my face. I wipe them away with the back of my hand. "That's pretty much all any of us can do, Mr. Gearly. Try to give back for what we've been given. Where will you go from here?"

"Dr. Adams recommended me to a surgeon he knows who specializes in weight-loss surgery. He thinks I'm a good candidate, and if I can lose fifty pounds on my own, he's willing to do the surgery."

"That's amazing," I say.

"It is," he agrees. "What's more amazing is that I think I can do it."

"I'm sure you can," I say.

Holden steps in beside me and says, "That's really great, Mr. Gearly."

"Wish I'd found the courage to do it a long time ago," he admits. "Maybe if I had, Charlotte could have had a chance to get help."

I don't know whether he is right or not, so I stay silent while the three of us absorb the implication. "There's no way to know," I say. "All we can do is go on from here."

"I guess that's what we have an obligation to do," he says. "Anyway,

I don't want you to be concerned about me any longer. I practically made my daughter a hostage in her own life because of the obligation she felt to me. I never want to do that to anyone again."

"It's not like that, Mr. Gearly."

"Even so, I've been a burden long enough. It's time I stand on my own two feet. Thank you for what you did. For getting me here and opening my eyes."

I can see that he is determined to live up to his words. And that it's time for me to say good-bye. "You're going to be fine," I say. And I know somehow that I am right.

"If you need anything, Mr. Gearly," Holden begins—

But he stops him with, "I know you mean that, and that still amazes me. But you two have lives to get back to. And that's what you need to do. I'll look forward to reading about your successes."

I touch his enormous shoulder and say, "You'll do great."

"Thank you, CeCe. For everything."

Holden takes my hand; we say a final good-bye and leave the room.

♪

MAMA IS COOKING when we get home. The wonderful smell of biscuits baking in the oven greets us at the door. Hank Junior and Patsy trot into the foyer, tails wagging hard at the sight of us.

Holden gives them each a rub, looking at me and saying, "I love your mom's cooking. Can she stay forever?"

"I'd be happy about it," I say, walking toward the kitchen. "We're home, Mama."

She smiles at the sight of us, smudges of flour on the green apron she's wearing. "Hey, you two. Hope you don't mind that I started dinner."

"Mind?" Holden says, walking over to kiss her on the cheek. "We don't want you to ever leave."

"Aww," she says. "You'd get tired of me eventually."

"No, we wouldn't," I say, putting my arms around her and hugging her tight. Somehow, I need one of her hugs right now.

She presses her hand to the back of my hair, saying, "Everything all right, sweetie?"

"Yeah. We just stopped to see Mr. Gearly. I think he's going to be okay."

"You've both been wonderful to him."

I shrug.

"You have," she insists.

"Maybe it's helping us get some closure," I say.

She wraps me a little tighter in her arms, kissing my hair. "Speaking of staying forever, I'm sure you're both ready to have your life back."

I pull back a little to look in her eyes. "Does that mean you want to go back to Virginia?"

"No. Actually, I wanted to get your opinion on something," she says, stepping back to look at us both with a suddenly serious expression.

"What?" I ask, instantly worried.

"Well, Case has asked me to marry him."

"What?" I can't hide my surprise.

Mama smiles then, and I can see how happy she is to tell us. "Oh, Mama, that's wonderful."

"It is, Mira," Holden agrees. "Really."

"Y'all don't think I would be foolish to hope I could keep a man like Case?"

I hear her doubts then, and even though I understand the source of them, I know how lucky Case is to have her.

"Mira," Holden says. "You're the best thing to happen to Case in a long time. I think he knows that."

"I just don't want to look like some aging desperado—"

"Mama," I admonish. "You are a beautiful woman. The woman Case Phillips fell in love with. He's been walking around with a broken heart for a long time. You two are meant to be together."

"You really think so?" she asks, clearly wanting to believe me.

"I do."

"I love him," she says.

"I know. I'm glad you're finally admitting it."

"So have you set a date?" Holden asks.

She shakes her head. "Case wants to get married right away. On the farm."

"And?"

"It seems too soon," she says. "After everything that's happened—"

I glance at Holden. He gives me a small nod. "Mama, we don't want you to wait because of us. I don't think we should put off living. We never know how that's going to go."

A flash of pain crosses Mama's face. "It seems wrong to be joyful when you've both lost so much."

"It's not," I say. "We live. That's our only choice."

Mama steps forward and pulls me into her arms again. "Will you help me get the wedding together?"

"Of course, I will. Is Aunt Vera coming?"

"I know she would love to."

"She'll stay here," I say. "We need something to celebrate."

"Thank you, honey. So much."

"I'm happy for you, Mama."

"Me too," Holden says. "Case is a lucky man. But then so am I."

♪

Holden

SO WHEN CASE said he didn't want to wait, he wasn't kidding.

The wedding is set for Saturday evening, less than a week from the day Mira told us he had popped the question. I don't blame them though. More and more, I'm beginning to believe that we shouldn't put off the things that really matter.

And it's been good for CeCe too. She's been busy with her mom and aunt, shopping for dresses, getting their hair done, planning the menu for the caterer. Case asked if we would be willing to sing at the wedding, and, after talking to Thomas, CeCe told him we'd be honored to.

We get together one afternoon with the band and rehearse the songs we'll be playing. We spend another couple of hours coming up with a set for Bartley's charity concert which will take place a week after the wedding.

CeCe surprises me with her focus on the music. She puts her all into it, and I realize what a professional she has become, putting the personal stuff on the back burner to the extent that no one would realize everything she has on her mind.

But I know. I catch glimpses of it when she thinks no one is looking. A sadness in her eyes that she won't acknowledge even to me. It's as if she's decided the only way to deal with what has happened is to put it away and forget that it actually did.

It's a solution that might work temporarily. Some things allow themselves to be put on the shelf for a bit. But I don't believe losing a child in the way we did will stay pushed down forever.

From my spot on the stage behind her, I strum my guitar through the last song of our set, closing my eyes to absorb her voice on each of the poignant words. *I want to live this life amazed. See the world like it's my very first day.*

That is the CeCe I've known and loved, the CeCe I married. Will she be able to look at life in that way again? I want to take her hand and lead her through her sorrow, shield her from the blows of grief.

But I can't unless she wants me to. Standing back when I see her in pain goes against everything I believe true of my role in her life.

"How's she doing?" Thomas asks when we're taking a break, before going through the set one more time.

I take a sip from a bottle of water and say, "If you ask her, she'll say fine."

"If I ask you?"

"I honestly don't know. There's just something different in her. This reserve. Something I can't quite put my finger on."

"CeCe's always been one to go after life wide open," he says. "When bad things happen to us, we get afraid to test the waters. You know that as well as I do."

"I didn't expect her to want to sing this soon. For the wedding or Bartley's show."

"Don't you think it's the best thing for her though?"

"Mostly."

"She'll find her way, Holden. You married a strong woman."

"I just don't want her to think she needs to get there on her own."

"Then tell her."

"I have."

"Give her time, Holden. She'll get through this."

I nod once because I want more than anything to believe he's right.

"On another note, I got the feeling you weren't too psyched about joining up with Bartley."

I shrug. "I'm sure it's a good opportunity."

"But?"

"I don't know. Not too sure I liked the way he was looking at CeCe."

"Jealousy? Seriously? That girl is as crazy about you now as she ever was. Not that I get it, mind you," he adds in a teasing voice. "Why would you worry about him?"

"He's a big star."

"So are you. You also happen to be her husband."

"Maybe I imagined it. I swear when I get up in the morning, it's like our lives got turned upside down and shaken to the point I'm not sure what's what."

"I know what you're feeling, Holden. But don't start looking for problems where they don't exist. Just be who you've always been for CeCe and she won't be looking to anyone else to be her hero."

"Thanks, man. I'm just being stupid, I guess."

"Hey, we all doubt sometimes. It's the nature of being a guy."

"You ever doubt Lila?"

"Early on, hell yeah. I might look like I have all the confidence in the world, but don't let the exterior fool you."

"You're full of it," I say.

"There he is. As long as you're giving me crap, I know you're gonna be okay."

I shake my head and land him a punch on the arm. "Let's get back to it."

"Oww," he says, protesting.

"Wuss."

"Jackass."

♪

CeCe

I'VE NEVER SEEN Mama so happy. Aunt Vera too. I think they're afraid to let me see it though. As if their happiness somehow takes away from what's happened to Holden and me. They'll be laughing when I walk in a room, and as soon as they see me, they stop.

Which is what happens on Thursday morning when I walk into the kitchen. They're drinking coffee at the table, laughing at something on Aunt Vera's phone. They look up, spotting me and go silent.

"Hi, honey," Mama says. "Would you like some coffee?"

"I'd love some," I say.

Mama starts to get up from the table, but I tell her I'll get it. I pour a cup and join them. "Can I ask you two a favor?"

"Of course," Aunt Vera says.

"What is it, honey?" Mama asks.

"Can you not feel guilty for being happy? You should be happy. And I'm happy for you."

Mama reaches across to take my hand. "I guess I do feel guilty. That maybe the timing isn't right."

"You and Case have loved each other for a long time. You shouldn't wait another minute to be together."

"She's right, Mira," Aunt Vera says. "We're kind of closing her out by acting glum every time she walks in the room. I'm sorry, CeCe. I didn't realize we were doing that. But you're right. We have been."

"I'm really sorry, honey," Mama says, stricken. "That's the last thing I meant to do."

"I know. It's okay. You're trying to protect me, but I need to be a part of it. The joyful part too."

Mama gets up and walks around the table to pull me in her arms. "I love you so much. Life is going to be good again. It will."

I hug her back, hard. I want to believe her. More than anything, I want to believe her.

♪

WE SPEND THE DAY getting a final fitting for Mama's dress. She looks so beautiful in it. "It looks like it was made for you, Mama. It couldn't be more perfect."

She runs her hands down the front, studying her reflection in the long mirror before us. "Really? Do you think I'll look pretty enough for a man like Case? There will probably be eight ex-girlfriends at the wedding."

"And is he marrying any of them?" Vera throws out with her typical candor.

I smile and say, "Good point."

"I'm just worried I'll look too old or too wrinkled."

"Stop," I say. "You're neither one of those. He'll be speechless when he sees you at the end of that aisle."

"I've never cared too much about being pretty," she says. "But I admit that on Saturday, I really would like to be."

"You are," I say. "And you will be."

♪

I HAVE AN appointment with Dr. McCormack at two, so I leave Mama and Aunt Vera at the boutique to finish up. I'm pulling out of the parking lot when my cell phone rings. I don't recognize the number, but pick up anyway.

"CeCe, it's Jacob Bartley. I hope you don't mind me calling your cell. I got the number from your manager. We go way back."

"Oh. Hi, Jacob. No, of course not. It's fine."

"I just wanted to thank you again for agreeing to do the show on such short notice. We were in a pretty bad bind."

"We're really happy to be a part of it," I say, intentionally putting the 'we' in there." But then I feel silly and add, "What can I do for you?"

"I was hoping you might be willing to meet with me to have another conversation about the orphanage in Belize. Maybe I'm mistaken, but I thought it seemed to strike a chord with you."

"It sounds like a wonderful place," I say. "What do you need?"

"Can we meet to discuss it?" he asks again.

I feel the alarm bell. I'd be lying if I said I didn't. But it's Jacob

Bartley, so I say, "I have an appointment downtown in a little over an hour. I'm near the Row right now."

"That's perfect. Meet me at the studio in ten minutes?"

"Sure," I say.

"Can't wait to see you," he says.

I click off then, wondering what kind of door I've just opened.

♪

CeCe

JACOB BARTLEY looks like a cross between Tim McGraw and Dierks Bentley. He's every bit as successful, and something in the way he carries himself says he's aware of it. He's waiting for me at the front entrance to the studio, his perfect white smile welcoming.

"Hey," he says, putting a hand on my arm and guiding me to his office. "Thank you for coming by. I didn't expect to get to see you again this soon."

"I'm glad it worked out," I say as we walk into the office. He closes the door behind us and waves me toward a long, red-leather sofa. I sit, and he sits down next to me, a couple of feet between us.

"So, I'll get right to it. I think you would be a wonderful ambassador for the orphanage. We need a strong female advocate for our fundraising. I'm hoping you'll be willing to be that woman."

I'm more than surprised, and I'm sure it shows in my expression. "I'm honored that you would ask, Jacob. But why me?"

"You have a big following. You're smart and articulate. And on a more shallow note, you're beautiful, and you catch people's attention."

"Wow," I say, more than surprised by the praise. "I'm not sure where you got your information—"

"My own two eyes," he says, something suddenly warm and sincere in his voice. He holds my gaze, and I don't think I'm imagining the flirtation there.

I shift on the sofa, crossing and uncrossing my legs. "I'm flattered, Jacob, but I'm sure there are plenty of other singers you could—"

"And I want you."

The words hang there between us. Is it my imagination that there's some other implication behind them? Do I venture out on that limb? Unless I do, there's no way I can continue this conversation. "Jacob. I'm married."

He watches me for a moment as if trying to decide whether he's going to join me on that limb. "Happily?"

"Yes," I say, unable to believe we're having this conversation. "I'm not sure how we got here."

He smiles a half–smile and shrugs. "I make no secret of the fact that when I see something I want, I go for it."

"Something?"

"In this case, a beautiful, talented woman."

"Who happens to be married."

"I know from firsthand experience those things don't always work out the way we want them to."

"You've been married?" I ask, giving in to curiosity.

"Way early on. Back before I got jaded. Caught her on the tour bus making out with my lead guitar player."

"That's terrible."

"It was at the time. That was before I made it. She was still trying to decide who to place her bet on."

"That's jaded," I say.

"And also true, unfortunately."

"I'm sorry."

"Don't be. Isn't that how we're purified? Trial by fire?"

I smile. "Your reputation is anything but pure."

He laughs. "You've been asking?"

"No," I say firmly. "The word's out anyway."

"I'm looking to be reformed."

"Did you just invite me here today for a flirt fest?"

He laughs again. "No, I didn't. I invited you here for the reason I gave you. Not to say I can't be sidetracked."

"You're incorrigible."

"Persistent too."

"I really am happily married, you know."

He studies me for a few seconds, as if trying to decide whether I'm telling the truth. "All right then, that being the case, can I talk you into joining me as an ambassador for the orphanage?"

"May I ask you a question?"

"Anything."

"What made you get involved there?"

He glances off for a moment and then meets my gaze directly. "I know what it's like to be an orphan. I didn't end up in the foster system until I was twelve. My mom had been in and out of jail for drugs. The last time she got sent away, it was for twenty years. She hit a family in a minivan one night when she was stoned and killed two people. There was no one else to take care of me, so I ended up with foster families. As you can imagine, no one wants to adopt a rebellious, red-neck teenager."

I start to say something sympathetic, but he stops me with a raised hand. "It's true. And that's who I was. On a positive note, those years made for a hell of a lot of good material for country music."

"You've written some amazing songs."

"Thanks. I appreciate that. So back to how I got involved with the orphanage. I was touring around with some guys after some shows we did in Central America, and we literally stumbled across the place. It was this small, concrete-block building, immaculately clean and surrounded by children playing and working around the place. The people who worked there invited us in and showed us around. All the kids looked happy and well-cared for. When they told us they were all orphans, I couldn't believe it. It wasn't anything like what I imagined an orphanage being like. We stayed for a couple of days and helped repair stuff, did some painting.

I know this might sound cheesy considering how lucky I've been with this career, but nothing has ever filled the hole for me the way that place did. I felt like I could make a difference there, and, to be honest with you, the main reason I'm grateful for what I've accomplished here is that it gives me the ability to help on a large scale."

"Wow, Jacob," I say. "That's an amazing story. Not what I would have expected."

"The player reputation and all?"

"Well, yes," I admit.

"I kind of like knowing I surprised you."

"It's admirable, what you're doing."

"Does that mean you'll join up with me?"

"It means I'll think about it. And talk it over with Holden."

"Fair enough. I'm going down the week after the concert. I'd love it if you could come too and check it all out. I'll be taking the jet down. Plenty of room."

"That's a really nice offer."

"Then I hope you'll take me up on it."

"Something tells me I should be a little afraid of you."

"If I had a woman like you, the last thing I would ever do is hurt you."

The words drop a blanket of heat over me, and I stand up quickly, saying, "I have to go. I'm going to be late for my appointment."

He stands too. "Sorry. I didn't intend for that to happen. You'll get back with me?"

I nod. "I have your number from when you called me."

"Cool. Thanks for coming by, CeCe. I really hope to hear from you."

"Bye," I say, leaving the office with quick strides even as I refuse to look back.

♪

DR. MCCORMACK IS waiting when I arrive at her office. She waves me past the check-in area, closing the door and walking over to her desk.

"How are you today?" she asks.

"Good," I say, still distracted by the meeting with Jacob.

"You look like you have a secret," she says, sitting in her chair and leaning back to look at me.

"No secrets," I say.

"Then tell me how you're really doing."

"Feeling a little lost, I guess."

"How so?"

"Like I was driving along for miles and miles, sure I knew where I was going, but someone changed the landscape, and now I don't recognize anything at all."

"You've experienced a terrible trauma, CeCe. Your feelings are completely understandable."

"But I don't want to feel like this."

"It's a process. A journey. And unfortunately one you have to travel through to come out on the other side."

"I understand that with my logical mind. I just don't want to do it."

"Because it's painful. Of course we're going to avoid pain. Part of being human."

"Being human sucks sometimes."

"It absolutely does. The only way to make it suck less is to throw yourself back into living. That's what gets us through. Finding things that make us feel worthwhile.

That's when I decide to tell her about Jacob Bartley and the orphanage. She listens intently as I describe the place as he had described it to me.

When I'm finished, she says, "That sounds like a perfect thing for you to be involved in right now. Are you considering it?"

"I think so, yes."

"What would hold you back?"

"Honestly?"

"Of course."

"I'm not sure what Holden will think. And Jacob Bartley is a pretty big flirt."

"I think you can handle that. Why would Holden not want you to go?"

"Just a feeling."

"Or maybe you're just looking for an excuse not to get involved?"

"Actually, I think I would like to be."

"Then be. This is the kind of thing you could throw yourself into for a while and do some healing."

"You think?"

"I do. Why don't you talk it over with Holden? I bet he'll be for it."

And by the time I pull into our driveway a couple of hours later, I've convinced myself she's right.

♪

Holden

I'VE SPENT MOST of the day writing in my office downstairs. My heart hasn't been in it for a while, but when I sat down with my guitar after CeCe left the house this morning, something inside me needed release. And the words and chords began to flow.

It's always been like that for me. Writing is catharsis. It's as if whatever hurt, pain, disappointment I'm struggling with on the inside can only find its way out on the backs of those words.

I write two complete songs. One that's just a feel good tune – "You, Me and a Palm Tree" – and another that gets to the heart of what we've been going through.

When CeCe walks through the door just before five o'clock, I'm just finishing up the last one. She comes into the office with Hank Junior and Patsy at her heels.

"Hey," I say.

"Hey," she says, walking into my arms and wrapping herself around me.

"How was your day?" I ask, kissing the top of her hair and breathing in its familiar scent.

"Interesting. How was yours?"

"Productive, actually. I wrote two songs."

She pulls back to look at me, surprise on her face. "That's amazing. Can I hear them?"

"Now?"

She nods. "Sure."

I pick up my guitar, sit in what I've designated as my writing chair and strum out the chords of the first one to refresh my memory. CeCe sits on the couch across from me, Hank Junior and Patsy hopping up to sit next to her. She puts her arms around each of them as I begin to sing the first song, a simple tune about getting away and remembering love in its first stages.

CeCe smiles when I'm done. "People will like that, Holden. It's a getaway song."

"Yeah," I say.

"Can I hear the other one?"

"Sure." I close my eyes and settle on the words, feeling their power, recognizing their truth. But it's not only my truth. It's CeCe's as well. When I open my eyes at the end of the song, I see the tears streaming down my wife's face, and my heart breaks a little.

I put down the guitar, walk over to the couch and drop onto my knees in front of her. "I'm sorry," I say.

She reaches out to run her hand through my hair. "Don't be. It's beautiful."

"Will it hurt every time you sing it though?"

"At first. But doesn't pain have to come before the healing?"

"I don't want you to be in pain."

"I don't want you to be either. But I know from this song that you are. It's okay to talk to me about it," she says.

"I don't want to add to yours."

"Sharing it with me isn't adding to it. I think it actually makes it a little easier for both of us to bear." She leans forward and wraps her arms around me, putting her head on my shoulder.

"Tell me about your day," I say.

"I went to the fitting with Mama and Aunt Vera. She looks beautiful in the dress. I can't wait for Case to see her."

"Did you have the appointment with Dr. McCormack?"

"I did. Before that, I actually met with Jacob Bartley."

At the name, I lean back a little, surprised. "Really? Why?"

"He called as I was leaving the fitting and asked if I could come by the studio. So I did."

"What did he want?" I ask, unable to deny the edge in my voice.

She meets my gaze as if she wants me to know she has nothing to hide and says, "He's asked me to be the other ambassador for the orphanage in Belize. He and a couple of the major donors are going there a week after the fundraiser concert."

"Oh," I say, completely unsure how to process this.

"I'd like to go," she says. "Would you be willing to come too?"

I try to keep my expression neutral when I answer, "That's kind of out of the blue, don't you think?"

CeCe shrugs. "I don't know. Is it?"

"What's involved in this ambassadorship?"

"Speaking to potential donors. Telling the orphanage's story to the media and other influential audiences."

"With Bartley?"

"Well, yes. That's all it would be."

I stand up and move across the room, putting my guitar back on its stand. "For you, maybe."

"Maybe? Holden. Are you serious?"

I draw in a deep breath, release it out slowly in an effort to resist coming across as a complete jerk. "I'm a guy. It didn't take much insight to see he has a thing for you."

"What if he does?" she asks. "Do you not trust me to handle it?"

"It's not a matter of trust."

"How can it not be?"

"Are you saying if the situation were reversed, you would be okay with it?"

"I'm saying I trust you."

"And I trust you."

"Then why is there a problem?"

I walk over to the window, fold my arms across my chest and stare out at the front yard of our house.

"Will you at least think about going?" she asks.

I don't know what else to say. "I'll think about it."

♪

CeCe

WATCHING MAMA WALK down the aisle on Saturday afternoon is a moment I will never forget. My whole life I have wanted her to have the happiness I've always known she deserves. She worked hard when I was growing up to make sure I had the things she wanted me to have, life luxuries like braces, that weren't a given in our household.

Her generosity and commitment to raising me the best she could made me forever determined to pay her back in whatever ways I could.

While I'm not directly responsible for her happiness today, I am thrilled that my life here allowed her to meet a man like Case, a man who adores her and sees her as special as I do.

I'm now standing at the front of the church with Aunt Vera next to me, Case on the other side, staring at the church doorway as if he cannot wait for Mama to appear.

When she does, we both gasp a little. Holden is giving her away. He looks unbelievably handsome in a black tuxedo.

Mama's dress is off-white and looks as if it was absolutely made for her. The sleeves are fitted and hit just above her wrists. The waist is narrow, and her figure would be enviable to a twenty year old. The top is simple but the skirt flows out and stops at her ankles. Her hair is pulled back into a simple knot at the nape of her neck. Her makeup is perfect, lipstick a soft shade of pink. I am almost unbearably proud of her.

I glance at Case. The look on his face tells me Mama has made a wise choice. Life is so full of ups and downs, peaks and valleys. Today is one of those days that make living through the valleys worthwhile.

♪

THE RECEPTION IS at Case's house. His band is playing out back, white tents lining the lawn under which enormous spreads of food make a mouthwatering display.

Mama and Case are at the head of the receiving line, and the guests file through to express their best wishes. Holden and Aunt Vera and I are at the end, and I really have no idea how they managed to organize everything so quickly and so well. Most of the people coming through I know, and I'm thankful that most choose not to comment on the tragedy with Charlotte Gearly. This isn't a night when I want to remember any of that.

Thomas and Lila arrive with Lexie. I lean down and give the little girl a fierce hug. She is so precious, and it always makes me feel full with happiness to see how crazy Thomas and Lila are about her.

"Hi, honey," Lila says, stepping forward to give me a warm hug.

"Hey, Lila," I say. "I'm so happy you're here. How are you?"

"Doing great," she says. "Thankful. How are you?"

"Better," I say, even as I'm not sure it's completely true.

"You look beautiful," she says. "And your mom. What a beautiful bride she is."

"I know. I'm so proud of her."

Thomas steps in and picks me up for one of his custom bear hugs. "Hey, gorgeous."

"Hey, you. You look presentable," I add, smoothing my hand across the lapel of his dark suit.

"He cleans up well, doesn't he?" Lila says with a smile.

Thomas leans over and whispers something in Lila's ear, which immediately causes her to blush. She swats him playfully.

"We better move on before we get in trouble with the groom," Thomas says. "See you at the table?"

"Make him behave, Lila," I say.

She shakes her head as if she knows better than to try.

Still smiling, I turn back to the line to see Jacob Bartley approaching. He smiles at the sight of me. I feel Holden's awareness of him in the stiffening of his shoulders.

A beautiful young woman has her hand wrapped through Jacob's arm in a proprietary gesture that makes it clear she considers him hers.

"Hello," Jacob says in his familiar country voice.

"Hi," I say, with some uncertainty, not having realized he would be invited to the wedding. But then again he and Case know each other, so I'm not sure I should be surprised.

Holden still hasn't said anything when Jacob looks to the woman on his arm and says, "Giselle Thompson. Holden and CeCe Ashford."

"Nice to meet you, Giselle," I say.

She smiles at me and says, "You too."

Holden says, "Pretty name, Giselle. Nice to meet you."

She meets his gaze directly and says, "It's nice to meet you, Holden. I love your music."

"Thank you," he says, the smile on his face the same one that makes girls on the front row of our concerts scream and throw lacy bras drenched in their perfume at him.

I slip my hand into his and look at Jacob. "We hope to have the chance to talk to you again in a bit."

"Of course," he says.

Giselle throws us both a smile as they walk on, and it's not my imagination that it lingers on Holden.

"Is this what we're doing now?" I ask once they're out of earshot, taking my hand from his.

"What?" he asks.

"Playing games."

He hesitates, as if he's considering denying it. But we respect each other more than that, and he says, "I'm sorry. It was a jerk thing to do. I guess I just wanted to give Bartley a taste of his own medicine."

"Or maybe you just wanted to flirt with Giselle."

He turns to me then, slipping his arms around my waist and giving me a sound kiss of apology. "Baby, I don't want any woman but you."

"And I don't want any guy but you. Are you sure you believe that?"

He nods, leaning down to kiss me with a soft heat. He pulls back and says, "Can you forgive me for being such an ass?"

"You're my ass," I say, smiling a little.

He laughs, and says, "As long as I'm yours, I don't mind being one."

And we turn to greet the next guests in line.

♪

CeCe

CASE PULLS ME aside, right before it's time to cut the cake later on in the night.

"Are you sure you don't mind me stealing your mama away for ten days?" he asks with a hint of apology.

"Of course not," I say. "She's so excited, but she's dying to know where you're taking her."

"I know. Think I should tell her?"

"It'll be a wonderful surprise. She's never been to the Caribbean. St. Barts is supposed to be amazing."

"I'm hoping she loves it."

"If she's with you, she will," I say.

"CeCe," he says quietly. "I'd like to promise you something."

"What's that?" I ask.

"I know I've earned myself something of a reputation over the years, and considering the way you and I first met, I'm surprised you'd let me anywhere near your mama. But I want you to know that I'll never hurt her. I can't believe I got lucky enough to find someone like her. I'll never take that for granted."

I step forward and put my arms around his neck, giving him a long hug. "I already know that. You two have found something special. And I think you're both going to protect that."

"Thank you for trusting me with her," he says.

"Thank you for loving her," I say.

Just as I step back, Jacob Bartley walks up and claps Case on the shoulder.

"Congratulations, Case. I think you hit the jackpot."

"Got that right," Case says, warmly shaking hands with Jacob. "Glad you could come."

"Thanks for the invite. What a great evening."

A woman in a red silk dress speaks to Case, and he turns to answer her, leaving Jacob and me standing side by side.

"Having fun?" I ask, feeling more than a little awkward.

"Yeah," he says. "Beautiful wedding. Great food. Incredible music."

"Where's Giselle?"

"Chatting up a record producer, I believe. She's working on her career."

"She's really pretty."

"Yes, she is."

"Are you two a thing?" I ask, and then wonder why I did.

"That depends," he says.

"On what?" As soon as the words are out of my mouth, I realize I've ventured into risky territory.

He smiles the smile that has melted countless female country music lover's hearts. "Do you really want me to say it?"

"No," I say quickly. "Jacob, you have to stop."

"Can I help it if I find you enchanting?"

"That's not a word I would imagine you using."

"It's not a word I've ever found applicable to anyone in my life before."

"I'm not in your life."

"But you could be."

"I think you're just entertaining yourself with me. Are you bored?"

"No. Right now, I'm anything but bored."

"And I'm married. Do I need to keep reminding you of that?"

"I'd like to think I could forget it, but sadly, no."

"If Holden sees you over here chatting me up, he might take a swing at you."

Jacob laughs a soft laugh. "Am I that obvious?"

"Yes, you are."

"Do you not think I could handle him?"

"He's got a good right hook."

"So I shouldn't test it, you think?"

"You shouldn't."

"He's possessive then?"

"He's my husband."

"And did you mention the trip to Belize?"

"I did."

He leans in close to my ear and says, "And?"

I lean away, start to make light of Holden's negative response, but something stops me. Maybe the fact that I've decided I really would like to go. Not because Jacob Bartley thinks he's infatuated with me, but for the reasons Dr. McCormack suggested. Because I feel the need to put myself into something larger than my own pain. With the hope that in doing so, I might start to feel hopeful about life again.

Just then, Jacob stumbles backward, barely stopping himself from hitting the floor. And then I realize it's because Holden has charged him like a bull defending his pasture from a stray opponent.

I scream. "Holden! Stop! What are you doing?"

But it's as if he doesn't hear me. He's pushing Jacob again, and they're rolling around on the floor like fourth graders fighting at recess. People are gathering around. Women gasp when they recognize Holden and Jacob.

Holden takes a swing. Jacob swears as Holden's fist connects with his jaw. I grab Holden's shoulders, trying to pull him off Jacob, but it's like trying to move a statue.

"What the hell?"

I recognize Thomas's voice and am so happy to hear it, I nearly sob. "Thomas! Make them stop!"

"Damn, boys, what the heck?" Thomas grabs each of them by the shoulder, holding them apart long enough to bark some sense at them. "Have you two lost your minds?"

"Stay out of it, Thomas," Holden says.

"And let you both end up in jail? I don't think so."

"What's wrong, Ashford?" Jacob taunts. "Can't handle a little healthy competition?"

"Your ego has clearly taken your brain hostage," Holden snaps, the last word slurring a bit at the edges. It's then that I realize he's had a good bit to drink. "What do you not understand about the word married?"

"I understand more about the word insecure."

"You son of a bitch!" Holden goes for him again, but Thomas makes a wall of himself between them, holding them apart.

"You two are making a right dumbass spectacle of yourselves," Thomas says. "Unless you want to see your twin mugshots on the front page of tomorrow's Tennessean, I suggest you each head to your corner of the ring."

Jacob wipes the back of his hand across his mouth, giving Holden a glowering look. "Yeah, and anyway, I need to find my date."

"I think you should have looked for her before you decided to come out here and hit on my wife."

Jacob shakes his head, looking at me and saying, "Talk later, CeCe?"

"Jacob, just go," I say, feeling the coiled tension in Holden and realizing he's ready to go after him again.

Jacob walks to the French doors that lead outside where most of the guests are. Thomas raises a hand at the few people milling around, looking shell-shocked and says, "Show's over, folks. Y'all join the party."

The spectators quickly leave then until it's just Holden, Thomas and me standing there.

"Brother," Thomas says, looking at Holden with a raised eyebrow. "What gives?"

Holden refuses to look at me, shaking his head and running a hand through his hair.

"CeCe?" Thomas directs to me.

"A misunderstanding," I say.

It's then that Holden does look at me, and I see that he is angry and more than a little drunk. "Misunderstanding?" he repeats. "What did I misunderstand? Was he or was he not all over you, CeCe?"

"No, he wasn't. We were just talking."

"Bullshit," Holden says, surprising me with the fierceness with which he says it.

"Obviously, someone's gotten the wrong idea somewhere along the line," Thomas says.

"I don't have the wrong idea. Bartley is moving in—"

"Stop, Holden," I say, angry now. "He can only move in if I let him. I'm not letting him."

"It didn't look that way from across the room."

"Maybe you're looking to see it that way then."

"Are you telling me he wasn't coming on to you?" Holden asks now, holding my gaze with his blue one, now hard as steel.

I start to deny it, but I don't want to be untruthful. "I can only tell you what I was doing. I'm not interested in responding to him in that way. Do I not have your trust?"

Thomas looks at Holden and says, "Man, she can't help what Bartley is thinking. Only what she does about it. And she's telling you she's not interested."

"I don't know what else I can say, Holden. I'm going to find Mama before she hears about this and thinks we've ruined her wedding." And I walk away.

♪

Holden

I FEEL THOMAS studying me with his questioning gaze. "Don't say it," I warn him.

"What? That you just acted like a donkey's behind? Okay. I won't say it."

I give him a look and drop onto the sofa behind me. "I'm not imagining it, Thomas."

"So he's got a thing for her. We can agree on that. But you can't go around starting fights. And you've got to trust your woman."

"I do trust her."

"Sorry. But it's not looking that way right about now."

"She's vulnerable, Thomas. With everything that's happened—"

"You're worried she's going to fall for the sweet talk?"

I shrug, miserable.

"You know her better than that."

"I know the CeCe before Charlotte Gearly. I swear I think he knows she's not in a good place, and he's using it to move in."

"Come on. Seriously?"

"I was talking to Case earlier, and he said Bartley called him up a couple days ago to congratulate him. They don't know each other that well, but Bartley hinted he'd like to come to the wedding, so Case invited him."

"Seriously?" Thomas says, frowning. "Jacob Bartley isn't someone who's lacking for social opportunities."

"I know. That's why I'm sure he wanted to come so he could 'run into' CeCe."

"You're sounding a little paranoid there, brother. And you know we've already committed to that concert with him. That ought to be a bucket of laughs now."

"So we cancel."

"We can't cancel. We signed a contract."

"Shit."

"Yeah."

I lean forward, elbows on my knees, regretting the Tequila shots I did with Case at the bar earlier. The room is starting to tip a little, left then right, maybe up and down. "What a mess."

"We just need to get through the concert, and that should be all of it."

"He's invited her to go to Belize with him and a couple other donors. He's asked CeCe to come along as an ambassador for the cause."

"Shit."

"Yeah."

"Maybe it's just that and nothing more."

I give him a look, and he says, "Okay, no."

"I guess when you're where he is in the world, you think you can take what isn't yours."

"Holden, we haven't done too badly ourselves, you know."

"Still, I don't look around at other men's wives, thinking I have the right to cherry-pick."

"Better hold up on that language, or you're going to make CeCe madder than she already is at you. And by the way, that's the next thing you have to fix."

I'd like to ignore him, pretend that he doesn't know what he's talking about, but unfortunately, he does. I stand, albeit, a bit shaky. "I need to find her."

"Hat in hand, buddy. Only way to get where you want to go."

I shake my head at him and say, "I'm on it," walking out of the room.

"Let me know how it goes," Thomas calls after me, and I feel sure this is one night when he's glad he's not me.

♪

CeCe

MAMA IS LOOKING at me with one of her worried expressions as I try to explain what happened in the house earlier without making her overly concerned.

"So you're saying Holden got into a fight with Jacob Bartley?" she asks, as if she can't imagine such a thing actually happening.

"Not really a fight," I say, reaching for words to put the whole thing into perspective. "Thomas kind of intervened."

"What was it about, honey?" Mama asks, shaking her head.

I guess the answer must show clearly on my face because she looks surprised, saying, "CeCe, is that Jacob Bartley after you?"

"He's harmless, Mama. And even if he weren't, I'm not interested in being unfaithful to Holden."

"And he knows that?"

"Of course he does. He's just — I don't know — since we lost the baby, we've both been having a hard time finding our way back."

Mama puts a hand on my arm, her eyes suddenly pleading. "Then you have to put aside everything else until you do. You have to protect what you have, CeCe, and when something is threatening it, you have to figure out how to deal with that. The love you two have for each other hasn't really been tested. It's easy to be in love when life is smooth sailing. What deepens it though is riding out the rough waves and finding your way back to what brought you together in the first place."

"I know, Mama. You're right. We're going to be okay. I promise. And anyway, tonight is about you. Let's not talk about this anymore."

Just then, Holden walks up, wearing an expression of apology. "Hey," he says. He leans over and kisses Mama on the cheek.

"If you heard about my moment of insanity, I hope you'll forgive me. I didn't mean to put a damper on your wedding day."

"Aw, honey, you didn't," Mama says. "But I sure would like to leave for my honeymoon knowing you two are all right."

Holden looks at me, and I know he's waiting for me to answer.

"We're fine, Mama. This is your night. And you need to get back to it. Isn't it time to cut the cake?"

"I think Case is looking for you, Mira," Holden says. "I saw him on the way through."

"Okay. Are you coming?"

"Yes, Mama," I say. "We'll be right there."

She leaves us standing together then, and I can't remember a time when this kind of awkwardness found its way between Holden and me.

"CeCe," he says. "I'm sorry."

I sigh, not sure what to say. "What were you thinking?"

"I guess I wasn't."

"I want to watch them cut the cake. Can we talk about this later?"

He runs a hand through his hair, looking impossibly contrite and gorgeous in his tuxedo. My heart flips over, and I wonder how he can possibly not know how utterly crazy I am about him. I start to say it, but something stops me. I want to, but I just can't seem to make the words come out.

I walk away without saying anything at all.

♪

CeCe

EVERYONE GATHERS outside the front of the house, waiting for Mama and Case to come out. A black limousine is parked and waiting, strings of cans tied to the bumper, courtesy of Case's band members. Holden is standing next to me, but there's a distance between us I've never felt before. I want to reach out to him, say something to make the distance go away, but I stay silent.

The front door of the house opens. Mama and Case step forward into the cheering guests who are now tossing pink rose petals at them. The scent of the flowers fill the air, and all of a sudden, tears are running down my cheeks.

Mama looks so incredibly happy. Aunt Vera is behind her, carrying her purse and another small bag. Their luggage is already waiting on the private jet Case has lined up to take them on their honeymoon.

Spotting me, she darts over and pulls me into a warm hug. "You'll be okay?" she asks close to my ear.

I nod. "Have the most wonderful time imaginable."

She pulls back and looks into my face, as if she's not sure she can believe me. I smile and say, "I mean it. Enjoy every moment."

Case is behind her then, leaning in to kiss me on the cheek and say, "I'll take good care of her, CeCe."

"I know you will," I say.

Case shakes hands with Holden. Holden hugs Mama and kisses her cheek, and then Case and Mama slide into the limousine, waving and smiling.

I love their happiness. It is a wonderful thing to see.

Holden reaches for my hand as we watch them pull away down the long drive leading to the main road. I lace my fingers through his, and we stand there without looking at each other, just renewing the connection.

Relief settles deep in my heart. I feel the apology in his touch, the seeking of forgiveness. I squeeze his hand, asking for it as well. He puts his arm around me, pulling me close. I'm instantly filled with a sense of belonging and rightness.

There are some things in life that are indisputable. Things we just know to the very core of our soul. The fact that I belong with Holden, regardless of the curves and potholes, is one of those things. I slip my arm around his waist and say, "Let's go home."

♪

Holden

NO ONE EVER said that commitment and marriage would be an easy road. I've decided that we humans are incredibly good at hurting one another and putting dents in our relationships that aren't that easy to smooth out again.

For the next two weeks after the wedding, I do my best to make up for my stupidity regarding Jacob Bartley. And CeCe does her best to put it behind us.

A couple of photos showed up on the Internet the day after the wedding. Jacob and me on the floor of Case's living room in what looked like a wrestling position. The PR skills of Jacob's team and our manager's skill with the press turned it into a fun-and- games kind of photo, squashing any rumors to the contrary.

I'm determined to focus on the part of the situation I know to be true, and that is CeCe's love for me. The past two weeks have been like a second honeymoon for us. We've stayed at home for the most part, focusing on each other, working on new songs. I feel closer to her than ever.

On the morning of Bartley's concert, we're lying in bed, talking quietly about the songs we're most confident about, going over the places where we're likely to have trouble, working out how to avoid it.

CeCe's head is on my chest, her hand on my mid-section, thumb rubbing back and forth as she talks. "Are you sure Thomas is okay with the new song? We haven't rehearsed it as much as the others."

"He says he's got it. You two are so in tune to each other with your singing. I think you'll hit everything exactly right."

"Thanks," she says. We're quiet for a minute or so, the morning sun dipping into the room through a crack in the curtains. "Holden?"

"Yeah?"

"Promise me you won't—"

"You don't have to say it, hon," I say. "I've learned my lesson."

"Even if he provokes you?"

"Even if."

"I just want this night to go off without anything bad happening."

"It will," I say. "Don't worry."

She slips on top of me, looking down into my face with a seriousness in her eyes that snags at my heart. "I'm yours," she says quietly.

"Yeah?" I say, running my hand through her long hair.

"Yes," she whispers, and then shows me that she means it.

♪

CeCe

IT'S BEEN A while since I've had stage nerves. But for the concert tonight at Warner Parks, I do.

I think we all do.

Holden and Thomas both are unusually quiet backstage. And I'm going through the songs in my head because I'm afraid I'll forget the words to our most recent.

Thomas is the first to speak, right before it's time to go out. "We've got this," he says. "For some reason, it feels like we're trying out the bike without the training wheels, but we're old hat."

"You're right," I say. "Holden, you good?"

"Let's do it."

We get the signal to head out just then, and, joining hands, we run on stage. The already cheering audience erupts with whistles and clapping. I pick up the microphone, and lead off with "Pleasure in the Rain." It's a crowd favorite, and a song I know without thinking. I see people on the front row singing along, swaying to the music, and I let myself go to that place I've always been able to find when I'm singing.

I don't know why I feared I wouldn't find it tonight. For the next hour, the music is all that matters. When I glance at Thomas and Holden, I can see that they've found that same place, where only the music matters, everything else forgotten for the moment.

We sing Holden's new song last. I close my eyes and hear it as he first sang it to me, the words giving me a clear glimpse into his heart and soul. The audience has gone quiet, hanging on the lyrics, swaying to its beautiful melody.

With the last note, the applause erupts. Thomas and Holden walk over to take my hands. We raise them high between us, calling out, "Thank you!" in unison.

The roar of the crowd is demanding an encore, but we were told Jacob had asked that we not do one. I catch a glimpse of him at the side of the stage. Thomas and Holden release my hands, Holden reaching for his guitar before leading the way off.

Thomas gives Jacob the thumbs up, but Holden ignores him. I smile and thank him. He stops me with a hand on my arm. "Do you know 'Walk Away'?"

The question catches me off guard, and at first, I'm not sure what to say. "Your song *Walk Away*?"

"Yes," he says.

"I do."

"Open up with me?"

I freeze, no idea what to say. "Jacob—"

"Come on," he says. "They'll love it."

I try to glance around him to check with Holden and Thomas, but Jacob has put himself directly between us. Before I can say another word, he's taking my hand and pulling me back onto the stage.

He's right. The audience goes ballistic at the sight of the two of us. His band hits the intro. Jacob picks up the microphone and takes the lead with the song. I wait for the chorus to join in. People begin clapping, and I realize I have to close out every other thought except getting through this song. I close my eyes and let the words rise up within me.

When we're done, Jacob leans over and kisses me on the cheek. "Ladies and gentleman, CeCe Ashford, my new ambassador for Orphan Relief Belize! I'd like to publicly thank her for opening her heart to this amazing cause. I hope she'll be joining us for a trip down there next week. We'll be updating the website with photos and stories of our experiences, so y'all be sure to check it out!"

The applause is deafening. I try to hide my surprise by smiling out at the crowd, waving and thanking the fans. Without looking at Jacob, I leave the stage.

♪

Holden

I SLIP OUT the back stage door, guitar case on my shoulder. I make a straight path for the Rover, pulse pounding at my temples.

Anger has a grip at my neck, and I know if I don't get out of here, I'm going to end up being arrested for assault. I asked Thomas to bring CeCe home, and he promised he would.

I get inside the vehicle, slamming my palm on the steering wheel. That son of a bitch! He'd planned that all along. Just like he'd planned getting an invitation to the wedding.

I drive straight home, resisting the urge to hit a local bar. Inside the house, Hank Junior and Patsy greet me, following me up the stairs where I throw on running clothes. Headed back downstairs I promise Hank I'll take him next time and let myself out into the night air.

I start running at a pace I know I won't maintain for long, but I need the burn as a release for the anger still boiling inside me. My shoes pound the sidewalk, my stride covering distance.

I run hard until drawing in breath is too painful to continue. I slow up, dragging in air but continuing on.

I run for several miles before rational thought begins to get a foothold. When I finally slow to a walk, it begins to occur to me what Bartley is doing.

He's trying to provoke me. He wants me to create a public scene in which he's the obvious good guy.

If I end up in jail, what better way for him to have a clear path to CeCe as well as public approval for it?

Could he be that conniving? That determined to have what he wants?

It's hard to believe he could, but that's what my gut is telling me.

My phone buzzes. It's a text from Thomas.

You all right?

Yeah.

I can't believe he did that. Asshole.

CeCe with you?

Yeah. We just got to the house. Where are you?

Out running.

Good for you. I don't know how you kept your cool. I'd be in jail right now.

I think that's what he wants.

Like he did that intentionally?

Yeah.

At least we're done with the concert.

I'll be at the house in five minutes.

I'll wait.

When I get there, Thomas is in the kitchen with CeCe. She's making coffee, her back to me. Thomas looks as if he's not sure what to say. I break the ice by walking over and kissing her on the cheek. She turns with a look of relief on her face.

"Hey," I say.

"Hey," she says, pressing her cheek against my chest and wrapping her arms around my waist. "I'm sorry."

"You didn't do anything wrong," I say.

"I know, but—"

"We don't have to see him again," I say.

Quiet hangs between us, and then Thomas says, "What about that announcement he made about CeCe being ambassador for the orphanage in Belize?"

"Maybe we can issue a press release saying I've decided not to accept for personal reasons," CeCe says.

"My guess is he's going to drag us through the mud if you do."

"So? He can't do this," CeCe says. "It's gone too far."

"Based on what we've seen, I'm thinking you'll be right, Holden," Thomas says.

"We'll recover. Anyone who knows us will realize I wouldn't back out lightly."

"He's got a pretty powerful PR machine," Thomas says.

CeCe shakes her head. "I can't believe he would use it like that."

"It seems pretty clear that he would."

"The only way I would consider going now is if you go with me, Holden."

I pull her closer, wrapping my arms tighter around her. "I don't think it's a good idea for me to go, babe. I might end up in jail in Central America."

"Then I'm not going either."

"That settles it," Thomas says. "We'll just ride it out. Right?"

"Right," CeCe says.

"Okay," I say.

Thomas slaps me on the back. "I gotta get home to my woman. Y'all hang tough."

"'Night, Thomas," CeCe and I say in unison.

When the front door closes, she pulls back to look up at me. "I'm so sorry."

I shake my head. "How'd you do with the surprise song?"

"I handled it, but that was pretty uncool of him. I could have made a great big fool of myself. I expected you to come out and beat him up."

"So did he."

"I'm proud of you for keeping it together."

"I saw red."

"And still walked away. You're such a grown-up."

I laugh a little. "Yeah, there's a positive, I guess."

"Want to go upstairs and let me show you what a good boy you were?"

"I'll be up as soon as I let Hank and Patsy out."

"Okay. I'll be in the bath."

I watch her leave the kitchen, realizing how incredibly lucky I am to have her. And that there's a line I'm not willing to let Bartley cross. Regardless of the cost.

♪

CeCe

THE NEXT MORNING, I go to an early yoga class at a studio downtown. I'm wound so tight I feel like I'm about to unspool in a million separate threads.

I slip into the class a few minutes after the start and place my mat at the back of the room. No one acknowledges the interruption, focusing on their own poses and meditation.

For the next hour, I slip into the peacefulness that yoga creates inside me. Once the class is done, everyone stands to roll up their mat, chatting softly in the relaxed aftermath.

I speak to several of the women I know, but then a tall blonde woman I've never met walks over, sticking out her hand. "I'm Octavia Matherson. You're CeCe Ashford?"

"Yes." I give her a polite smile. "Nice to meet you."

"I was at the concert last night. You were wonderful, and I just wanted to tell you how great I think it is that you're serving as ambassador for the orphanage in Belize. My husband and I are trying to adopt, so it's a subject dear to my heart."

I start to tell her I won't be doing it, but something stops me, and I just say, "I hope that will happen for you soon."

"Me too," she says. "It's such a long process, and when you've been waiting for a while, it gets kind of unbearable. Especially when you've had miscarriages."

I try to prevent pain from flashing across my face, but judging from her stricken expression, I don't think I'm successful.

"I'm so sorry," she says, putting a hand in my arm. "That was thoughtless of me, when yours was so recent."

I take a step back. "I really have to be going."

"Good luck with the trip to Belize," she says.

I leave the studio, feeling guilty for my abruptness with her. I know she didn't mean any harm, but I still haven't gotten used to my personal life being such an open book.

At the car, I get inside and sit for a moment with the engine running.

I feel suddenly angry at Jacob for creating this situation and putting me in the middle of it.

Just then, my cell rings. I glance at it and see his name on the screen. I start not to answer, but my current state of anger overrules common sense.

"I'm surprised you found the courage to call me," I say.

"You're mad at me?" He sounds genuinely surprised.

I drop my head against the seat, close my eyes. "Did you expect me not to be?"

"Maybe temporarily."

"It's not temporary, Jacob. You've put me in a horrible position."

"It doesn't have to be."

"It is. I really don't want to talk to you."

"Give me one minute."

"I'm counting."

"I received a call yesterday morning from the director of the orphanage about a little girl who was born to one of the teens there. Sadly, the young girl died after childbirth. The baby has a hole in her heart, and they are asking me if there is any way to get her to the United States for the surgery she is going to need. It's going to take some incredible diplomacy to get her out of the country. I'm thinking you're the girl for the job."

I stay silent for several long moments, letting his words sink in. I'm so unhinged by the picture he's just painted that I can't think what to say.

"CeCe? Are you still there?"

"I—yes. That's horrible, Jacob."

"It's tragic for sure. But I think we have a chance to right something here. Give this little girl a chance at life. I've already been in touch with a surgeon at Vanderbilt who is willing to take on her case."

"I don't really see how I can make a difference here, Jacob."

"You're a celebrity with a positive reputation and that will bring credibility to the baby being in the best hands possible."

"You'll understand if I'm a little suspicious of your motives."

"So I have a crush on you. I'm not making a secret of that. But this isn't about me. It's about a baby girl who might not live if she doesn't get this opportunity."

I hear the sincerity in his voice, and all of a sudden, I feel shallow for making this about me. "When are you going?"

"We would need to leave tonight. I assume you have a current passport?"

"Yes, but tonight?"

"Will you come, CeCe?"

"I can't give you an answer right now, Jacob."

"Then call me by one o'clock. If you can't, I'll go on without you. I'm just not sure I'll be successful."

And with that he hangs up.

I put my phone in the passenger seat, hardly knowing what to think about first. The fact that a newborn baby needs this opportunity. Whether I really can make a difference or if this is another ploy by Jacob to put my marriage in jeopardy. And too, what will Holden say? Would he be able to trust that Jacob is telling the truth?

I don't have definite answers to any of my questions. And I don't think there's any way I'm going to.

♪

Holden

I'M IN THE backyard throwing a Frisbee for Hank Junior when CeCe gets home. She walks out on the terrace, clapping when Hank catches it. He spots her and immediately drops the Frisbee to run and greet her.

She drops onto her knees, and he covers her face with kisses. "Hey," she says, looking up at me with something just short of a smile.

"How was yoga?"

"I'm loose," she says.

"Maybe I should take it up too."

"You'd definitely cause a stir in class."

I walk over and slip my arms around her waist, leaning in to kiss her neck. "Would I cause a stir in you?"

She leans back to look up at me. "Always."

I kiss her, and then pull away, sensing there's something she wants to say. "What is it?"

"Can we talk?"

"Sure."

I take her hand and lead her to the bench at one corner of the terrace. We sit down.

"What is it, CeCe?" I ask.

She looks down at her hands, then forces her gaze to mine. "I'd like to go the orphanage in Belize. There's a newborn there who needs to come to the United States for heart surgery. Jacob says I can help make that happen."

Something inside me collapses a little. "Did you see him this morning?"

"He called," she says softly, as if she doesn't want to cause me pain. "The teenage mother who had the baby died. Jacob thinks it won't be easy to get permission for the baby to come here for the surgery. He thinks I might be able to persuade the officials. I would like to do this, Holden. And when I get back, we can go away for a while. Find an island somewhere. Just you, me and that palm tree."

I fold my arms across my chest and watch Hank Junior and Patsy as they scout the fence line. I don't say anything for a long time, processing what she's said, considering my response.

"I love you, CeCe," I finally say. "And that means I have to be willing to let you go, even if I'm afraid you'll never come back."

"I will," she says. "I promise."

"Don't promise," he says. "But if you do, I'll be waiting."

I get up from the bench then and walk away, leaving the woman I love to find her own way back to me.

♪

Next: *Nashville: Part Ten*

Nashville – Book Ten – Not Without You

THE NASHVILLE SERIES
BOOK TEN

not
without
you

RITA® AWARD WINNING AUTHOR

INGLATH
COOPER

Get in Touch with Inglath Cooper

Email: inglathcooper@gmail.com
   Facebook – Inglath Cooper Books
   Instagram – inglath.cooper.books
   Pinterest – Inglath Cooper Books
   Twitter – InglathCooper

Books by Inglath Cooper

Swerve

The Heart That Breaks

My Italian Lover

Fences – Book Three – Smith Mountain Lake Series

Dragonfly Summer – Book Two – Smith Mountain Lake Series

Blue Wide Sky – Book One – Smith Mountain Lake Series

That Month in Tuscany

And Then You Loved Me

Down a Country Road

Good Guys Love Dogs

Truths and Roses

Nashville – Part Ten – Not Without You

Nashville – Book Nine – You, Me and a Palm Tree

Nashville – Book Eight – R U Serious

Nashville – Book Seven – Commit

Nashville – Book Six – Sweet Tea and Me

Nashville – Book Five – Amazed

Nashville – Book Four – Pleasure in the Rain

Nashville – Book Three – What We Feel

Nashville – Book Two – Hammer and a Song

Nashville – Book One – Ready to Reach

On Angel's Wings

A Gift of Grace

RITA® Award Winner John Riley's Girl

A Woman With Secrets

Unfinished Business

A Woman Like Annie

The Lost Daughter of Pigeon Hollow

A Year and a Day

About Inglath Cooper

RITA® Award-winning author Inglath Cooper was born in Virginia. She is a graduate of Virginia Tech with a degree in English. She fell in love with books as soon as she learned how to read. "My mom read to us before bed, and I think that's how I started to love stories. It was like a little mini-vacation we looked forward to every night before going to sleep. I think I eventually read most of the books in my elementary school library."

That love for books translated into a natural love for writing and a desire to create stories that other readers could get lost in, just as she had gotten lost in her favorite books. Her stories focus on the dynamics of relationships, those between a man and a woman, mother and daughter, sisters, friends. They most often take place in small Virginia towns very much like the one where she grew up and are peopled with characters who reflect those values and traditions.

"There's something about small-town life that's just part of who I am. I've had the desire to live in other places, wondered what it would be like to be a true Manhattanite, but the thing I know I would miss is the familiarity of faces everywhere I go. There's a lot to be said for going in the grocery store and seeing ten people you know!"

Inglath Cooper is an avid supporter of companion animal rescue and is a volunteer and donor for the Franklin County Humane Society. She and her family have fostered many dogs and cats that have gone on to be adopted by other families. "The rewards are endless. It's an eye-opening moment to realize that what one person throws away can fill another person's life with love and joy."

Follow Inglath on Facebook

at www.facebook.com/inglathcooperbooks

Join her mailing list for news of new releases and giveaways at www.inglathcooper.com

CPSIA information can be obtained
at www.ICGtesting.com
Printed in the USA
LVHW091653180821
695554LV00008B/1071